PIPER DAVENPORT

Road To

DESIRE

DOGS OF FIRE BOOK #1

COPYRIGHT

Cover Model
Dylan Horsch

Photographer
Golden Czermak

Cover Art
Jack Davenport

TRIXIE
PUBLISHING

ISBN-13: 9781705625125

DOGS OF FIRE

For the man who inspires me daily!
I love you, baby.

ONE

Danielle

I STARED DOWN at my dashboard console and willed the check engine light to stop the infernal red glow. How I got where I was, I had no freaking clue, which meant I had no freaking clue how to find the freeway entrance to get home. "You are an idiot, Dani," I whispered out loud.

As if on a mission from the devil, my nineteen ninety-nine Honda shuddered, then back-fired, slowing to a crawl as I inched forward down a non-descript side street. Why Portland didn't have better signage was beyond me.

I jumped as my cell phone pealed in the silence of the car. Without looking at the screen, because really, I was trying not to end up dead in some obscure place I'd never been before, I flipped it open. "Hello," I whispered.

"Why are we whispering?" Kim, my best friend of more than ten years, whispered back.

I cleared my throat and took a deep breath. "I'm kind of lost and my stupid car won't go over nineteen miles an hour."

"So, no different than any other day," she quipped. "How did the date go?"

"Sucked."

"How bad?" she asked.

"Getting my eyeballs plucked out by crows, while my fingernails were ripped off one-by-one would have been much more enjoyable kind of bad," I ground out

"Ew, sorry honey," Kim commiserated. "Did you stay and have dinner with him?"

"No. I endured one drink and an appetizer and then faked a phone call. Seriously, Kimmie, the guy was a douche."

"So, online dating's not for you?"

"Dating, *period* is not for me."

Kim chuckled. "Where are you?"

"I have no freaking clue," I admitted. "Somewhere in Arbor Lodge I think?"

"Holy crap, girl, you don't want to be lost there when it's almost dark."

"Thanks, Captain Obvious." I leaned forward to get a better view out of the windshield. "It's totally deserted, and I can't find a street sign to save my life."

"What's around you?"

"Nothing." I squinted trying to make out the light in front of me. The area was heavily commercial, so I wasn't sure what business would be open past eight on a Wednesday night. "I think I see something. Crap. My contacts are killing me."

"Pull over and take them out, silly. You have your

2

glasses with you, right?"

"Yeah, but I don't want to stop, Kimmie… what if I can't get started again?"

"What if you can't see what you're about to hit?"

"Stop being so logical," I ground out.

Kim sighed. "Please, Dani, be safe. Pull over, put on your glasses, and call your brother."

"Fine. I'm pulling over. Hold please." Guiding my car to the curb, I put it in park. "Okay. I'm gonna hang up and call Elliot."

"Good. Call me when—"

The phone went dead.

"Crap." I took a second to pull out my contacts and slide on my glasses, before I glanced in my side mirror and put the car in drive again. "Okay, old lady, please get me somewhere I can find a phone." I inched out into the street again and rolled about three hundred feet before my car let out a sputter and a hiss and the engine died. "Okay. It's okay," I chanted. "We've been here before, girl. You can do it." I cranked the engine and although it turned over, I couldn't get it to fully engage. I tried again, got it started, but had barely pulled further to the side of the road when it died...again. "No, no, no, no!" I cranked the engine again, but still no luck, so I put it in park.

Grabbing my purse off the floor, I rummaged around for my phone charger, finding it and plugging it into the lighter, hoping for enough juice to call my brother. I pushed every button on my phone in an effort to power it up again, but it had been losing its charge quicker and quicker over the past few weeks and it was now officially dead. "Damn it!"

I dropped my head to the steering wheel and took a minute to feel sorry for myself as I imagined the six-o'clock news headline, "*Young woman murdered after car breaks down in sketchy area of Portland. It's surprising since she comes from law-enforcement royalty. Another statistic? It certainly looks that way.*"

I'm not entirely sure how long I sat in my dead car and imagined my murder and death before a knock at my window had me squeaking in fright. I glanced out to see an extraordinarily gorgeous man leaning down with a sexy smile on his face. Tall with darkish hair, blue eyes, and a face that could only be described as beautiful, he looked quite a bit like Charlie Hunnam with a full beard and nose ring. He wore a pair of faded jeans that looked like they were made for him, a white thermal, tight-fitting shirt that showcased his muscular chest a bit too well, causing my heart to race and my breathing to catch. A black leather jacket that cemented his sexy as hell look completed the ensemble.

I cranked my window part of the way down... he couldn't kill me if he could only get his fingers inside, right?

"You lost, darlin'?" he asked.

His voice washed over me and I squirmed in my seat as I tried not to sigh at the slight southern twang. "Um, yeah. A little."

"Not a great part of town for a pretty girl to get lost in." He straightened, crossing his arms. "You got someone comin' for you?"

I squeezed my eyes shut and shook my head. "Both my car and my phone are dead. So, that would be a big fat no."

"Alright. Why don't you come with me?"

"No, that's okay."

He smiled again. "Sweetheart, my club's yard is right down the block. I'll get some of my brothers to push your car into the lot where it'll be safe, and we can fix it for you tomorrow. In the meantime, you can get out of the cold and either make a phone call or I'll take you home."

I bit my lip and pondered my options. The definite probability of dying of starvation and exposure before morning, or the potential of being murdered by the best looking man I'd ever seen were pretty much all I could come up with.

"No one will hurt you, if that's what concerns you," he promised.

"I wish that made me feel better," I admitted. "I mean, I wonder how many women have gone off with some tall, gorgeous man because he said he wouldn't hurt them, only to be murdered? Super murdered. We'd never know, right? 'Cause they're dead. Like as in dead, dead, not a little dead, but a lot dead."

His mouth quivered for a second before he burst out in laughter. "You've got a point, darlin', but if you're with me, no one'll touch you."

"Including you?"

He sobered, but his eyes were still sparkling with humor. "If that's what you want."

I rolled the window back up and grabbed my purse and keys. I had a feeling I'd regret this sudden trust I was feeling toward him, but I didn't really have much of a choice other than to let him help me, so I unlocked my door and climbed out of the car.

He held it for me and slammed it closed once I was on the sidewalk. I'd locked it before he closed it, not that it mattered... no one would steal a piece of crap car like mine and I kept nothing of value in it.

The wind had picked up since I left the restaurant, and I pulled my coat further around me as we walked down the street. "I'm Danielle, by the way. Um, Dani, actually."

"Booker."

"Nice to meet you, Mr. Booker."

"Just Booker."

"Oh. Okay."

He smiled.

"You mentioned your club's yard." I frowned. "What kind of yard?"

"This location's our wreck 'n' tow yard. Got other businesses in other locations," he said vaguely. "Anything with an engine, we can tow, fix or build."

I nodded. "And you said 'club.' I'm assuming it's not a sewing club, right?"

Booker smiled. "Motorcycle club."

I stopped. It took him a minute to realize I was no longer beside him, which gave me a partial view of the back of his jacket. Dogs of something. Dogs of Wonder? No, that wouldn't be right... a badass motorcycle guy wouldn't have Dogs of Wonder on the back of his jacket.

Well, crap!

He walked back toward me. "You okay?"

"Motorcycle club?" I asked.

He nodded.

"Like Hell's Angels?"

Booker smirked. "In theory."

"Crap." I glanced up at him. "I really should go."

"Go where, darlin'? There's nothing around here for over a mile in any direction."

"Clarify something for me. Are you a club because you have really nice bikes and like to hang out and drink beer on occasion, or are you like outlaws or something?"

"Since that's club business, it's none of yours."

"Right." I couldn't seem to stop swallowing convulsively. "Just point me in the direction of the closest place I can make a phone call and I'll get out of your hair."

"About twenty-five yards in front of you."

"You don't understand," I whispered. "I can't go in there."

"Why the hell not?"

"Because my dad's the freakin' chief of police," I snapped, before realizing I'd just spouted off something that could get me killed or kidnapped in a heartbeat, depending on whose hands that information was in.

"You're shittin' me."

I shook my head. "I wish I was."

"Well, fuck me."

"No thank you," I quipped. Retorts were my specialty, especially when I was nervous.

He cocked his head. "You wouldn't be disappointed, babe."

I pressed my lips into a thin line, willing my mouth to stay shut.

Booker chuckled. "The shop's clean, sweetheart. Totally legit, although, probably better I take you home than you have your daddy pick you up."

"It would be my brother, actually... or Kimmie. Kim's my best friend. Not that you care who my best friend is." I took a deep breath, rambling was not a good option right now.

He smiled again. God, he had a nice smile. Of course, it was the panty-dropping kind, but for now, I wouldn't react...my undies must stay firmly in place. "There's only six of us here right now, so we'll get your car into the lot, get your info, and I'll take you home."

I swallowed. "I should call my brother."

"Then we'll get your car into the lot and you can call your brother."

I nodded and let him lead me through a large parking lot surrounded by eight-foot high fencing complete with barbed-wire on top. I followed him into the warmth of a sparse but clean waiting area. It looked like the waiting room in my local oil change place, which for whatever reason surprised me. I'm not sure what I was expecting. Maybe centerfolds from Playboy circa 1984 plastered on the walls?

"Phone's on the counter," Booker said. "Dial nine for an outside line."

I nodded and picked up the phone, dialing as he opened a door and yelled, "Mack! Need you in the front."

"Hello?" Kim answered, sounding confused.

"Kimmie, hey it's me," I whispered.

"Ohmigod, Dani!" I could hear the sounds of the restaurant she worked at in the background. "I was worried sick. I take it your cell phone died again?"

"Yeah." I glanced to my right and could see Booker talking with someone across the room out of earshot. "It's officially dead, dead."

"Where are you calling me from?" she asked.

"Um, some wrecking place I managed to break down in front of."

"Of course you did," Kimmie said with a chuckle. "Did you call Ell?"

"Um, I can't."

"How come?"

"The shop is owned by a motorcycle club," I whispered, and glanced at the door again to make sure Booker wasn't listening.

"So?" she whispered back.

"Hello, I've seen that Sam Crow show... they're not entirely above board."

Kim burst out laughing, the tell-tale snort indicating she was unable to control her mirth.

"Kimmie," I snapped.

"Ohmigod, Dani, you are precious. Truly," she said, and laughed again.

"Oh, shut up," I ground out. "You know if I call Elliot, he'll get all—"

"Dani? Keys, babe," Booker demanded.

I jumped a little because I hadn't seen him walk back over to me. "Um, hold on a sec," I said to Kim, and rummaged in my purse. Winding the car key from the rest of my keys, I handed it to him, and he nodded then left me again. "Okay, I'm back."

"Who was that?" Kim asked.

"One of the men who works here."

"Um, he knew your name and he called you babe," she

8

pointed out. "I'm thinking you're being purposely obtuse."

"His name's Booker," I said.

"He sounds delicious."

"Meh," I lied.

"Call Elliot, Dani. Or I can come get you when I get off in an hour."

"No," I said with a sigh. "I'll call Ell."

"Good. Borrow his phone and call me when you get home, okay? I've gotta grab my orders."

"I will." I was midway through dialing my brother when Booker returned, so I hung up and forced a smile.

"You call your brother or friend or whoever?" he asked.

"Kim. Yes. She's still at work. I was just about to call my brother."

"Why don't you do that and then you can give me some information while we wait for him."

I nodded and picked up the phone again. I got his voicemail. "Hey Ell, it's me. I broke down in Portland and was wondering if you could come get me. I'm at...," I glanced up at Booker for assistance, and he handed me a card. I rattled off the address and phone number of Big Ernie's Wreck 'n' Tow, and then hung up again. "Voicemail."

"Picked up on that, babe," he said.

My cheeks heated. "Right."

Booker stepped behind the counter and handed me a piece of paper with Big Ernie's logo on it. "Write down your address and phone number and I'll call you when we know what's wrong with your car."

"Are you planning to wreck it?"

He smiled and shook his head. "We'll tow it over to the auto repair shop and fix it there."

"One of the other businesses, I presume?"

"Yeah."

I nodded. "I won't be able to answer, but you can leave

a message and I'll call you with a good number."

He nodded and I scribbled down my information. I couldn't imagine what the repairs on my car would be, but as a kindergarten teacher, I could pretty much guarantee they'd be out of my budget. I jumped again when the phone rang... I was seriously wound up with nerves that only a bottle of merlot was going to come close to calming.

"Big Ernie's," Booker said, and then smiled at me. "Yeah, she's here."

He handed me the phone. "Hello?" I said.

"How the hell did you end up at a scrap yard in Arbor Lodge?" Elliot demanded.

I watched distractedly as Booker and three other men walked outside and toward where I left my car.

"No clue," I admitted. "I was in the Pearl and thought I was going toward Vancouver, but I guess not."

"For someone so smart, your sense of direction is pathetic."

"Yes, I'm well aware," I grumbled.

"Where's your phone?" he asked.

"Dead." I sighed. "Like as in dead, dead."

"I'm buying you a new one."

"You don't need to do that," I argued... for the umpteenth time.

"I know, sis, but your stubbornness is starting to mess with my schedule," he said.

I smiled. I loved my brother, even when he was annoying. "Starting to?"

He chuckled. "I'm in the middle of something; can you hang out for a while?"

"No, it's fine. I'll grab a cab."

"Which will cost you the same as a phone," he said.

"Point taken big brother." I wrinkled my nose. "I greatly thank you for your astute observation."

"Grab a cab to the station and I'll drive you home from

there."

"No, it's fine. I'll head home."

"Dani," he said with a sigh.

"Elliot," I mimicked, and smiled. "Seriously. It's all good. I promised I'd call you and I called you. I might work with five-year-olds, but I'm not one, so don't worry."

"Oh, you're funny. Are you sure you're okay?"

"Yes, I'm fine. Swing by later if you want. I'm just going home. I have to be at work early tomorrow, so it'll be an early night for me."

"How about I grab you a burner and then I'll order you a decent phone later."

"Thanks, Ell. I'll pay you back," I said.

"We can argue about that later. I have to go."

"Okay, 'bye." I hung up and slipped behind the desk in search of a phonebook.

TWO

Danielle

"**Y**OU NEED SOMETHIN' darlin'?"

I jumped (again) and turned to find myself practically chin to navel with the very large man Booker had been speaking to earlier. I looked up and grimaced. He was blond with deep blue eyes and he looked intense.

"Hi. I'm Dani."

"Hi, Dani," he said, and smiled.

"Hi," I repeated, stepping back for space, but only managing to run into the lip of the desk. I refused to wince in his presence, but I did bite the inside of my cheek hard enough to draw blood.

"You said that."

"Um, yeah. I did. Great observation skills." *Ohmigod, he is not a five-year-old. Get it together, Dani.* "Um, sorry if I wasn't supposed to be back here, I was looking for a phonebook."

"You're looking for a phonebook," he said, and stepped closer to me.

"Yes. A phonebook. Do you have one? I need to call a cab. Can you back up a bit, please?" I mean, really. Where the hell was I going to go? He'd just boxed me into a corner. I took a deep breath.

"You need to call a cab," he said, his voice low and raspy.

I let out a frustrated sigh. "Yes, I need to call a cab."

"What about an Uber or a Lyft?"

"My phone's dead," I explained. "But even if it wasn't, it's too old for the app, and my brother can't pick me up. He's still at the station." Why did I feel the need to offer so much information?

"Station? Like a train station?"

"No."

Mack frowned. "As in police station?"

Crap!

I bit my lip. "Will you please let me by? You're making me nervous and all I want to do is call someone to pick me up and take me home."

"I'll take you home," Booker said as he walked back inside, a scowl on his face directed at "big biker man" in front of me. "And get the hell away from her, Mack. You can see she's freaked."

"Did she tell you her brother's a cop?" Mack demanded.

"Detective, actually," I corrected and then dropped my head. I needed to shut the hell up.

"Move the hell away from her," Booker repeated. I took a minute to look at him and his expression was a little scary. He gave his friend a look like he would kill him if he didn't do as he said. Instead of making me nervous, it made me feel protected. Another clear indication there was something inherently wrong with me.

Mack grinned, raising his hands in surrender as he stepped away from me. I skittered around the desk and back out in the open, keeping my purse in front of me… for what I'm not sure. I just felt a little protected somehow.

"Come on. I'll take you home," Booker said.

"No, it's okay. If you can just call me a cab, it'll be fine."

Booker shook his head. "We're closed, darlin', and it'll take a while for a taxi, so let me just take you home."

I swallowed.

"What?" he asked.

I glanced at Mack and then back at Booker. "Um… aren't bikes really dangerous?"

Booker seemed to share another secret look with Mack before they both burst out laughing.

I pulled my purse closer. "Well, if you're going to stand there and laugh at me, then I definitely want to call a cab."

Apparently, I'm freaking hilarious when I'm scared out of my ever-blessed mind, because Mack laughed harder.

"I've got my truck," Booker said, once he'd sobered.

"With or without a shovel and a tarp in the back?"

Booker frowned. "What?"

"Nothing. Never mind." I figured if he was going to murder me there wasn't a whole hell of a lot I could do about it at this point. "Yes, a ride home would be much appreciated."

Booker nodded and waved his hand toward the roll-up door.

"Nice to meet you," I said to Mack, and headed outside.

"You too, babe," Mack said to my back.

Booker led me to his Ford F-150, and I turned to face him. "Can I borrow your phone please?"

"What?"

"Your phone. May I borrow it for a second?"

He reached into his pocket and handed it to me. "Knock yourself out."

I stepped in front of the truck and took a photo of it, along with the license plate, texting the photos to Kim so she'd know who was driving me home and when I was leaving. At least if he did murder me, they'd be able to track down my killer.

"Thanks," I said, and handed the phone back to him.

He smiled his sexy smile again and pulled open my door. I wasn't expecting his gallantry as he waited for me to climb inside, but I covered my surprise. I didn't realize badass biker men did that kind of thing.

Booker climbed in beside me and started the engine while I buckled up. He didn't say anything as he guided the truck away from Arbor Lodge and I took a moment to take in his ride. It was new with all the bells and whistles, so to speak. Leather seats, wood inlay, and a kick-ass stereo system... at least it looked like a kick-ass stereo system. It was currently off.

About ten minutes passed and I had about all the silence I could handle. "Your real name's not Booker, is it?" He glanced at me and shook his head before focusing on the road again. "Are you going to tell me your real name?"

"Austin Carver."

"Oh," I said, unable to hide my surprise.

He smiled. "Not what you were expecting?"

"Not really, no. Don't get me wrong, it's a nice name. Sweet sounding, but I guess I expected you to be Maverick or something like that."

"Maverick?"

"What's wrong with Maverick?"

"Only a pussy would ever go by Maverick."

"What if that's the name his parents gave him?" I challenged.

"Then, if he weren't a pussy, he'd change it."

I bit back a smile. "I won't tell Maverick's mom you said that."

"You know a Maverick?" he asked.

I nodded. "He's one of my kids. I teach kindergarten."

"Fuck me. Of course you do," he grumbled, and pulled onto the freeway.

I gathered my purse close to me again. For some reason, the fact he didn't seem to like my choice of employment bothered me. It shouldn't. He didn't know me, and he was probably a criminal for Pete's sake, but I was the one who felt embarrassed.

"What's your group's name?" I soldiered on, my inability to stay silent when I was nervous working against me.

"My group?" He raised an eyebrow.

"Your club. Whatever."

He studied the road again. "Dogs of Fire."

"Why did you pick that?" I asked.

"I didn't."

"Why did your group... I mean, club, pick that?"

Booker shrugged. "Don't know."

"You don't know why they picked it?" I studied his profile and saw his jaw lock. "Sorry, not my business."

He neither agreed nor disagreed.

"Do you need my address?" I was unbelievably desperate for conversation, apparently.

"I have it."

"Right," I mumbled. Of course he did. I'd written it down for him. I studied him again. God, he was beautiful. I licked my lips and focused back on the road. "So, do you work at Big Ernie's?"

"Sometimes."

"So, it's not your regular job?"

"No."

"You're obviously not a mechanic," I mused.

"Why do you say that?"

"You're too clean," I blurted out. "I mean, your hands aren't caked with black oil and stuff. Sorry. Never mind. It's none of my business."

He chuckled.

"What's so funny?" I demanded.

"You don't like silence, do you?"

"I like silence… just not when I'm nervous. Crap. Never mind. Ignore me."

"Babe, I've been trying to ignore you since the second I saw your piece of shit car crawling down my street," he said.

I gasped, my irritation rising to dance with my nerves. "Well, you didn't need to come and rescue me. I didn't ask you to." He chuckled again and I blinked back tears, feeling both angry and insecure at the same time. "I'm sorry if my talking bugged you. I was just trying to be friendly," I continued, because, seriously, I was obviously a glutton for punishment. "It's what nice people do when other people help them. They ask them about their life and find common ground in an effort to make conversation."

"Is that what they do?" he asked.

"Typically, yes," I whispered, and turned toward the window.

I managed to keep my thoughts to myself as we drove into Hazel Dell and down the private driveway into my apartment complex. Not the greatest part of town, but also not the worst. It was what I could afford and it worked for me now.

"This is me," I said, pointing to the stairway that led to my second-floor unit.

He nodded. "I'll walk you up."

"You don't need to do that."

"I know," he said, and climbed out of the truck.

Gathering my purse, I pulled my jacket closer around me and pushed open the door. Booker stood on the other side and, again, waited for me before closing the door and walking me upstairs. I unlocked my apartment door and pushed it open, flipping the light on before stepping inside.

"Thank you for everything," I said.

"I'll call you tomorrow or Friday about your car."

Crap, right. I was going to have to pay for my stupid car to be fixed. "Yes. Um, I forgot to ask. Do you take credit cards?"

He frowned, but then nodded his head. "Yeah, babe, we take credit cards."

I relaxed. "Okay, good. Thank you. Well, it was nice to meet you, Austin. Thanks again for everything."

He gave me a chin lift in response and turned and sauntered down the stairs. I know for a fact he sauntered, because I leaned out my front door and watched him leave. His long, muscular legs and perfect butt made me sigh, and I realized he probably heard me, so I ducked back inside and closed and locked my door, leaning against it to catch my breath.

* * *

Booker

I was fucked. Royally fucked. The second I saw the pretty little blonde trying to force her car down the street, I'd known I'd help her. Couldn't really stop myself. She was gorgeous. Petite, curvy, big tits, nice ass, and she smelled incredible, but it was the glasses that sent me over the edge. I could envision her in thigh-highs, pearls, and those glasses while she straddled and rode me.

When I'd coaxed her out of her car and she'd started talking, her obvious sense of humor showing even though

18

she was terrified, I'd watched in fascination as every emotion she was feeling showed on her face in real time. I couldn't remember ever meeting a woman more beautiful... and fucking innocent. Kindergarten teacher and daughter of the chief of police. Shit.

I dialed Mack's number and then started my truck.

"Yo."

"You got the car over to Hatch's?" I asked.

Hatch Wallace was our Sergeant at Arms and owned his own shop close by. We took all of our more difficult jobs to him because he was a genius with engines.

"Yeah," Mack said. "It's fucked up. Might need to rebuild the engine."

"Shit." I headed onto the freeway. "I'll be there in twenty."

I hung up and stared out at the road in front of me trying to figure out how the hell I was gonna get out of this, and whether or not I really wanted to.

THREE

Danielle

MY BELL RANG an hour after Booker left. I opened the door to my brother who leaned down to kiss my cheek as he handed me a box with a phone inside and stepped into my apartment. My brother was tall, just over six feet, with blond hair and hazel eyes. My girlfriends all had crushes on him, waxing poetic about how much he looked like Brad Pitt.

"Hi," I said, and closed the door.

"Hey. Where's your car?" he asked. "It's not in the lot."

"One of the guys at the wreckage place is having it towed somewhere to evaluate it. He's going to call me tomorrow or Friday." I glanced at the new phone. "Well, he's going to leave me a message and I'll call him back since he can't really call me."

Elliot chuckled. "Got it, sis."

"I forget you're smarter than you look." I grinned. "Want some wine or a beer?"

"I have to go, actually. Just wanted to make sure you got home safe. What time do you have to be at school tomorrow?"

"Seven."

"Want me to pick you up?"

"Oh, yes. Crap. I didn't even think about how I was getting to work," I admitted. "I'm a little frazzled."

He crossed his arms. "How was the blind date?"

"Ohmigod, it sucked. So bad. He was boring with a capital B. He went on and on about the mating life of silkworms."

"You'd be well-dressed."

"I'd be dressed in stuff that was dry-clean only. Pass," I retorted.

Elliot chuckled. "I could set you up, you know."

"No," I said quickly. "I'm done for now. I just want to focus on getting my life back and maybe saving again."

My brother's face darkened. "Asshole."

"Yes, I know, Ell, but there's nothing we can do about it. Em did all she could legally and he's making restitution."

Our sister, Emily, was a lawyer and had been trying to deal with my issues from a legal standpoint for years.

"A hundred bucks a month is bullshit."

"I agree. I'm hoping Emily can find more in his financials."

Elliot studied me for a few tense seconds. "Okay, I'm going. I'll pick you up tomorrow at six-thirty."

"Thank you. You're the best big brother on the planet."

He grinned, his body relaxing a bit. "Don't I know it."

He gave me a quick hug and then he was out the door, and I locked up and flopped onto the sofa. I pried open the plastic wrapping containing the flip phone, plugged it in, powered it up and called Kim.

"This is Kim."

"Hey, it's me."

"Well, hello 'me.'" Kim giggled. "Got your text. Brilliant."

"Thank you," I said.

"I assume you're home and safe?"

"No, I'm buried alive in a ditch on the side of the road."

"Oh, where? I'll come rescue you."

I laughed. "I love how you've always got my back."

"I'm a giver," she retorted.

"On that note, can you give me the number I texted those pictures from, please?"

"Ah, sure? But you have to tell me why."

"One of the guys said he'd call me tomorrow with an update on my car and I want to give him the new number."

"Hmm-mm, I bet you do," she said. "Tell me the real reason."

I both loved and hated that my best friend could see right through me. "That *is* the real reason."

"Is he hot? Your 'the guy' that's 'one of the guys'?"

Ohmigod... was he hot? That was an understatement. "He's a thug, Kim."

"That's not what I asked."

"Yes, he's good looking... in a rough sort of way, I guess."

"Hmm-mm, right," she retorted. "I'll text it to you."

"Thanks."

"Do you need a ride tomorrow?"

"You're willing to come and get me at six-thirty?"

She gasped. "In the morning? Ah, no. Sorry, I just don't love you quite that much."

22

I giggled. "I know. Ell's picking me up."

"Oh, how I love him."

"I know, babe. Everyone does."

"Okay, I'm gonna text you his number and then hit the hay."

"Thanks, Kim. See you on Tuesday for lunch, right?"

"Definitely. 'Bye."

"'Bye."

I sat on the sofa staring at the phone for what seemed like an eternity before Kim's text came through. The number popped up on my screen and my heart raced in excitement. It was just after ten and I was typically in bed by now and wondered if he might be too. Maybe he wouldn't answer, and I could leave a message. I bit my lip. I didn't really know what to do. I felt compelled to call him. Like if I didn't hear his voice before I went to bed, I wouldn't be able to sleep.

"Dani, you are ridiculous," I told myself, but it didn't negate the fact that I was attracted to him. In a big way.

I set the phone aside and sipped my wine, then picked the phone up again and stared at it. I set it aside again and repeated these actions for several minutes as I contemplated my stupidity. In the end, I chalked it up to the fact that he had my car and I was just calling him to give him information. It didn't matter that it was past ten on a Thursday night. It was business, so I dialed the number.

"Yo."

"Um, hi. Is this Austin?" I asked. No response, so I glanced at my phone, then put it back to my ear. Maybe I'd dialed wrong. "I'm sorry. I must have the wrong number."

"You got me, Dani." His voice washed over me and sent a chill down my spine.

"How did you know it was me?" I asked.

He chuckled. "No one else calls me Austin."

"Oh. Right. Um, I just wanted you to have my new

number for when you know what's wrong with my car."

"And you had to tell me that now?"

I was officially an *idiot*. "Well, no, I guess not. But it was either now or really early in the morning because I have to be at work at seven and I figured if you were asleep, you wouldn't answer so I was going to leave a message. I didn't expect you to pick up." Crap, I was rambling again.

"Got it, darlin'."

"Well, good. Okay. I'll let you go."

"Probably a good idea."

I should have hung up. But as always, I was a glutton for punishment. "Why is it probably a good idea?"

"Dani, I'm not the man for you."

I gasped. "Excuse me? I never said you were."

"You don't have to say it out loud, babe. It's written all over your face."

"It is *not*! Wow. Are you always this rude, or am I just lucky?"

He chuckled and damn if I didn't squirm a little at the sound. "Your car's a piece of shit."

"I'm guessing it's both," I grumbled.

"You really shouldn't be driving it," he continued, ignoring my astute observation.

"Well, it's all I can afford, so I don't have much choice in the matter."

"Why is it all you can afford?"

"Um, excuse me, Sir Rude-a-lot, that's none of your business."

He chuckled again.

I sat up straighter. "Well, have someone call me with how much it's going to cost me to fix it and I'll have someone drive me down to pick it up."

"Four-thousand, seven-hundred, ninety-two dollars is the current estimate," he said.

I choked. "What?"

"Your engine's pretty much shot, Dani."

"I don't have that kind of money," I whispered, blinking back tears. I tended to get a bit emotional when I was exhausted.

"Pickin' up on that, darlin'. Wonderin' why."

I dropped my head back and stared at the ceiling. "If you must know, an ex stole my savings and my identity. I have spent the last four years trying to clear my name and get him prosecuted, and now I'm lucky enough to get a hundred bucks a month in restitution. He apparently spent the money he stole... or more likely, hid it... and spent thirty days in county. Bonus, he got three years' probation. I, on the other hand, have a credit rating that's in the toilet and have to use the credit card my daddy gave me in order to deal with emergencies, which this certainly is; however, I don't really want him having to pay five-grand for a car that's not even worth that much." I groaned. I couldn't believe I'd just shared all of that with a virtual stranger, particularly because outside of my family and the asshole who stole my money, Kim was the only other human being who knew the story. "Sorry. Too much information."

"How much did he steal?" Austin asked...no, demanded.

"I'm sorry?"

"How much did the asshole steal from you?" He sounded angry.

"It's not important," I whispered.

"Dani. How much did he steal?"

"Fifty-four thousand, six-hundred, seventy-eight dollars and sixteen cents," I blurted. "And that's just what he took out of savings. He charged another sixty-grand to credit cards he opened in my name."

"Fuck me. Seriously?"

"Seriously. I'd been saving for a house." I felt tears slip down my cheeks as the memories of Steven's betrayal flooded back. "Anyway, it's not your problem. Um, I'll talk to my dad and figure out what to do about my car. I really appreciate all your help. I'll talk to you tomorrow. 'Bye." I hung up and shoved my face into a throw pillow to scream. I didn't have long to wallow in self-pity when the phone jingled in my hand. "Hello?"

"What was the bastard's name?" Austin demanded.

"Excuse me?"

"The asshole who stole your money. What's his name?"

"Why?"

"Babe, what's his name?" he repeated, his voice pitched low.

"Steven."

"Steven what?"

"No one."

"Dani, give me his fucking name."

"No," I stressed. "It's none of your business." I heard him take a deep breath and then there was a knock at my door. I frowned. "I should go, there's someone at my door."

"Yeah, you should open it, darlin'."

"I'm not opening my door at ten o'clock at night, Austin. Despite my persona, I'm not an idiot."

He chuckled. "Open it, babe."

I frowned and rose to my feet, making my way to the door, and peeking through the peephole. I hung up with a sigh and opened the door. "What are you doing here?"

Austin's eyes did a full sweep of my body, and then he smiled and slid his hand to my neck. Pushing me further into the room, he kicked the door shut and leaned down to cover my mouth with his. He stroked my pulse as his other arm wrapped tightly around my waist and pulled me tight against him. His tongue pressed against my lips and I opened for him, my heart racing, my knees weak, and all I could do was grip his jacket and hold on for the ride.

It took a minute for me to come back to reality, and to

my utter horror I remembered what I was wearing. Dark blue camisole with a shelf bra that did nothing to support my overly large breasts, a pair of ratty plaid pajama pants, my hair pulled into a messy bun on top of my head and not a stitch of makeup. I hadn't brushed my teeth, probably had nasty wine breath, and here I was kissing the hottest guy on the planet who I'd just met less than three hours ago.

I pushed at his chest. You know, the one that felt like granite under my fingertips? He didn't budge, so I pushed again.

"Not done, baby," he said, smiling against my lips.

"But you need to be," I whispered, admittedly, somewhat half-heartedly.

His hand slipped to my cheek as he leaned back and frowned. "Didn't feel like I needed to stop, darlin'."

I licked my lips and nodded. "But you do all the same."

Austin stepped back with a smile.

I crossed my arms over my chest in an effort to hide the effect he had on my body. "What are you doing here?"

He shrugged as his eyes swept my apartment. "Nice place."

"Thank you."

"You live here when the asshole stole your money?"

I shook my head. "No. I had to move out of my other place. This place is *way* cheaper."

"And you don't want to live at home?"

"No," I said. "I'm not running to my parents because I made an error in judgment. They raised me to be independent and being an adult means life sucks sometimes. They do what they can, which I'm very grateful for, but I need to work this out on my own."

"How did you manage to get this place?"

"I know the owner."

His eyes came back to me. "Meaning?"

I sighed. "Meaning, he knows I'm good for the rent, so he waived the credit check."

Austin scowled. "Tell me his name."

"The manager?"

He stepped toward me. "No."

I rolled my eyes and tried to put distance between us. My back hit the wall of my tiny foyer. "I'm not telling you Steven's last name, Austin."

He gently grabbed my arm and pulled me back toward him. "I'm not leaving here until you do."

I smirked. "Hope you like sleeping on a couch, then."

Austin gave me his panty-dropping grin again. "Your bed'll do just fine."

"You are *not* sleeping in my bed, Austin."

He chuckled. "We'll see."

"What are you doing here?" I asked again, trying to ignore his thumb stroking the pulse on my wrist.

"No fuckin' clue."

"We're back to rude, I see."

He laughed. "Shit, you're funny."

"I wasn't trying to be funny."

"I know, baby."

I couldn't stop a shiver. "Don't call me 'baby.'"

"You like it."

"Doesn't mean you should do it," I challenged. "You're gorgeous, you know you're gorgeous, but the fact remains, I don't know you and I don't really know why you're here."

His smile grew. "I'm gorgeous, huh?"

"Poor choice of words, apparently."

"Let's stop talkin', then." He leaned down and kissed me again, and I couldn't do anything about it. Don't get me wrong, I could if I'd wanted to, but let's be honest, I had never been kissed like this, let alone looked at the way he looked at me. He wasn't anyone I would have thought would find me attractive. I was far more school librarian than biker chick and typically only received interest from nerds.

"What's his last name?" he asked when he broke the kiss.

"Mills," I answered, my eyes still closed, my breath still labored. "Crap!" I snapped when I came to my senses and looked up at him. He was once again grinning. "I mean, Millson," I improvised.

"Nice try." He stroked my cheek. "I'll see you soon."

"You will?"

He nodded. "'Night, baby."

He kissed me one more time and then walked out the door, leaving me standing next to the door in shock. I closed the door, locked it, and grabbed my wine on my way to the kitchen. After dumping the glass, I dialed Kim.

"Hey, lady."

"Ohmigod."

"What?" she asked.

"You're never going to guess what just happened." I filled her in on my entire night, including details about Austin "Booker" Carver.

"He just showed up and then gave you a mind-blowing kiss?"

I nodded and realized she couldn't see me. "Yes. Two," I said… well, whispered with breathy desire is probably a better description. "Maybe three."

"And he's like a biker dude?"

"Yes." God, *again*, breathy desire. I was losing it.

"Oh, honey, you're screwed."

"Crap? Am I?" I asked.

"Why did he want Steve's name?"

"No clue, Kimmie. But he seemed pissed. Which is weird because he doesn't know Steve… or me."

Kim hummed, but didn't say anything further.

"What?" I demanded.

"I think you've got a man who has decided to claim

you."

"What?" I asked. "What does that mean?"

"I think you should have Elliot check this guy out."

"Kim! Stop speaking in riddles." I shoved my wine glass in the dishwasher and slammed the door a little harder than I should have. "You know I'm not good at this kind of stuff."

"Just have your brother do a background check on him, Dani. Then go from there."

"Why do I need to get Elliot involved in this?"

"Will you just listen to your best friend and know that she is looking out for you?" Kim asked. "You've only ever been with one guy and he kind of ripped you off, so you're both naïve and gun-shy in the face of hot guys."

"I'm not a child, Kim," I pointed out.

"I'm not saying you are, Dani. But you're sweet and you see the good in everyone. You even give Steve somewhat of the benefit of the doubt most of the time."

"I do not."

"You do too," she argued. "It's your only vice."

I snorted. "Suck it, Kimmie."

"Oooh, if only I could."

"You and your oral sex fixation."

"Hey, I enjoy fellatio," she said.

I groaned. "Kim—"

"Well, you seem to object to me saying I love giving head—"

"Oh, gross. Kimmie, please!"

"Just talk to your brother."

"No." I made my way into my bedroom and set my alarm. "This man isn't interested in me. He's probably just trying to see if he can trick me into sleeping with him. But I'm too smart for him. I'll talk to my dad about the repair costs, then go from there. I'll probably never see him again."

"Okay, Ms. Oblivious. We'll see."

"Yes, we will. I love you, but I have to go to bed. I have a million things to do tomorrow and it's way past my bedtime."

Kim laughed. "Okay dear, sweet, innocent friend. Love you too."

"'Night."

"'Night," Kim said, and hung up.

I brushed my teeth, climbed into bed, and closed my eyes, but all I could see was Austin's face in front of me, smiling and leaning forward for a kiss. I rolled over and tried again, but this time, Austin's head was on the pillow next to me.

"Crap." I flopped onto my back and dragged my hands down my face. Glancing at the clock, it said eleven-thirty and I groaned. Six hours. *If I can fall asleep right now, I'll get six hours of sleep.*

I glanced back at the clock at midnight and this continued until I finally fell asleep around two. By the time the alarm sounded, I was sure I'd only managed a twenty minute power nap, so I snoozed. The problem was I snoozed until six a.m., which meant I was still rushing around my apartment when my brother arrived to pick me up. Lucky for me, he didn't grill me about why I was so tired. After I told him what time to pick me up, he dropped me off at school and went on his merry way. Thank God for small favors.

FOUR

Danielle

FRIDAY AFTERNOON, I laid the last piece of paper in the last stack of grading I'd been putting off for a week and sat back in my chair. Checking my watch, I groaned. I was probably the last person left in the school and with another early morning, I was exhausted. But at least now I was caught up and could enjoy my weekend.

Opening my desk drawer, I grabbed my purse just as my new phone jingled. I found it buried in the bottom of my bag and answered it without checking the ID. "Hello?"

"Hey, babe."

I frowned. "Austin?"

He chuckled. "Your car's fixed."

"But I haven't had a chance to talk to my dad yet." I

rubbed my forehead, my sleepless nights and money worries manifesting themselves into a wicked headache. "I have to see if he's okay with the amount. Don't most places have to get authorization to do repairs beforehand? What if I can't pay for them? Crap, Austin, I don't know if I can pay you. I thought you were going to call me yesterday. I need more time to figure this out."

"Babe, take a breath," he said.

I did, but found I needed to take a few more.

"The car's fixed," he continued. "No charge."

"What? What do you mean, 'no charge'?"

"Generally, it means that currency in the form of money won't be exchanging hands."

"You're funny." I couldn't stop a smile. "But the sad fact is that I don't have five-thousand dollars and I don't really feel comfortable asking my dad for it. He's bailed me out too often over the past few years."

Austin sighed. "Babe. It's covered."

"Explain to me exactly how it's covered. What do you want in return?"

"We can talk about it when I drop your car off."

"I knew it," I snapped. "Forget it. You can keep it."

I hung up and threw my phone in my purse, my sleepiness leaving my body faster than it had arrived. Seething, I grabbed my purse and jacket, and headed out of my classroom through the outside door. I locked up, passed by the office, and waved to the janitor who was grabbing the trash from the front of the school.

I needed to walk. My apartment was about three miles from the school and not having a car was a good excuse to walk off my anger and maybe a few calories as well. I'd been lazy of late and had gained close to thirty pounds after Steven's betrayal. I needed to stop feeling sorry for myself and do something about my weight. I texted my brother and told him I didn't need a ride again and then headed toward home.

The temperature had dropped since lunchtime, so I zipped up my coat, shoved my hands in my pockets and put my head down against the wind. I had gone about a block when I regretted my decision to walk home in the cold.

I no longer wanted to lose weight. I wanted to soak in a hot tub with a glass of wine. This thought brought to light the fact that I didn't have a tub worthy of soaking anymore, which then reminded me I also didn't own a car anymore, which led me down the rabbit hole of anger and irritation at the drop-dead gorgeous man who'd interrupted my plan. I was getting my life back... at least I was trying to, but now Austin wanted to mess with that plan. I had to figure out a way to come up with the money without asking my dad.

The large fir trees that lined the private drive leading to my apartment came into view and I sighed with relief. I was home. I would call my brother and work out a game plan. He'd know what to do.

I turned down the road and quickened my steps. I was now officially freezing and wanted to get inside and wrap myself in a blanket. The parking lot came into view... and so did my car. I stopped walking, confused. Movement out of the corner of my eye had me turning to see Austin climbing from his truck.

He frowned. "Did you walk home, Dani?"

"Huh?"

"Did you walk home? Alone?"

I looked up at him. "Um, yeah. I don't have a car."

"Fuck." He shook his head. "Did you walk yesterday as well?"

"No, my brother has been driving me, but—"

"Here." He reached into his pocket and pulled out my car key.

I shook my head. "I can't pay for it, Austin."

"Take the key, Dani." I did and he swore again. "Babe,

34

your hand is like ice."

"Generally happens when it's cold."

"You don't own gloves?"

"I didn't bring them, on account of the fact I didn't expect to be walking home," I admitted.

"Why didn't you call me?"

"Why *would* I call you?"

He took both of my hands in his and rubbed them together. "I would have picked you up."

"Why would you have picked me up?"

Austin frowned again. "Let's get you inside."

"Wait," I said, trying to pull my hands from his. He just held them tighter. "What are you doing here?"

"Babe." He looked at me like I was touched in the head. "I'm bringing you your car."

"I feel like you and I are having a huge failure to communicate," I grumbled.

He waved his hand toward my apartment. "Let's talk inside."

"You're coming inside?"

"Not talkin' to you out here in the cold." He gave me his sexy smile. "'Course, we don't have to talk at all. Up to you."

I let out a quiet huff. "I don't know what you want from me."

"Come on. Let's get you warm," he said.

I had a feeling he wasn't going to leave, so I nodded and led him upstairs. Unlocking the door, I stepped inside and turned on the light. Austin closed and locked the door behind us and I shrugged out of my coat. He threw his jacket on the chair by the television, but kept his vest on.

"Why don't you talk like a thug?" I blurted out.

He chuckled. "I'm sorry?"

"Nothing. Just ignore me." I dropped my purse on the chair by the door. "Do you want some wine?"

"Got beer?"

"Um, maybe. I'll look." I stepped into the kitchen to see if Elliot had left anything the last time he'd come for dinner. I pushed the milk to the side and found three bottles of my brother's favorite Portland brew, hoping Austin would like it. I grabbed one, opened it, and then poured the last of the red I'd been drinking over the past few days into a glass.

I walked back into the living room to find Austin lounging on my sofa, his booted feet up on my coffee table, television remote in his hand, flipping through stations and looking like he owned the place. He smiled at me and reached out his hand to take the beer. "Thanks, babe."

I handed him the bottle and shook my head as I sat in the chair next to the sofa.

"What are you doing?" he asked.

"What do you mean?"

He patted the cushion next to him. "Come here."

"Um, no, I'm good right here. Thanks," I said, and sipped my wine.

"Babe, come here."

"No."

He dropped his feet to the floor and he twisted to face me. "No?"

I nodded and then shook my head.

Austin grinned, setting his beer on the coffee table and rising to his feet. He took my wine and set it next to his beer.

"What are you doing?" I asked, leaning back as though I could achieve some space. Silly me.

He reached down, sliding one arm under my knees and one behind my back, lifting me like I weighed no more than a small child, and sitting back on the sofa, me in his lap.

"Austin?" I squeaked.

"Yeah, babe."

"*What* are you doing?"

"Well, I *was* drinkin' a beer." He stroked my hair, grinning like a loon.

I tried to scoot off his lap, but he held me tighter. "You are really confusing me."

"I get that."

"Then why are you doing it?"

He chuckled. "Because it's fun."

I sighed. "Will you take payments on my car?"

"No."

"I can't pay you without making payments, Austin."

He ran a thumb over my lower lip. "I know."

I pushed his hand away. "Are you expecting me to sleep with you?"

"Not because I fixed your car, no."

"What?"

"Babe," he said with a sigh. "We're working shit out here. I want to get to know you, so we're gonna get to know each other."

"Because *you* want to get to know *me*, we're going to get to know each other?"

"Yeah."

"What if *I* don't want to get to know *you*?"

He sat up a little and kissed me. Captivated me with his mouth. It was awesome... and terrifying, and yet, I couldn't do anything but feel, so I did. And it was overwhelming and beautiful and all-encompassing. He kissed me like he was drowning and I was his breath.

I came to my senses and broke the kiss, dropping my forehead to his. "What are you doing to me?"

He smiled, kissing me quickly again. "What do you *want* me to do to you?"

"I think it would be best if I didn't answer that."

Austin ran his thumb over my lower lip again. "Damn, you're cute."

"Are you really not going to let me pay for the car?"

"I'm really not going to let you pay for your car." He

gave me a gentle squeeze. "Mack thought it was worse than it was. Hatch looked it over and said it would take less than three hours."

"Five grand's pretty bad, Austin."

He grinned. "If you were someone off the street, it's what we'd charge you. The parts were less than three hundred. The rest was labor."

"I should at least talk to the person who fixed it about payments. Hatch, was it?"

"*I* fixed it, Dani."

"You did?" I glanced at his hands. They were still void of oil.

He smiled. "I wore gloves, babe."

"I thought you were using "I" in the general sense of you organized it," I said.

"Pickin' up on that."

I took his face in my hands. "You fixed my car."

"I fixed your car."

"Thank you."

"You're welcome."

"Can I get off your lap now?" I asked.

"In a minute."

I didn't say anything, but I liked that answer. I liked where I was. He made me feel protected.

"You asked me a question before," he said.

"Which one?" My face heated.

"My use of language."

"The thug comment?"

He chuckled. "Yeah, that one."

"I'm sorry. That was rude."

"Would you like me to answer it?" he asked.

I shrugged. "If you want to."

"We're gettin' to know each other, right?"

I nodded. "Can I get off your lap now?"

He shook his head and my heart raced. He was delicious.

"Can I at least have my wine, then?" I asked. He grinned, gripping me tighter as he leaned forward and lifted the wine glass off the table, handing it to me. I smiled. "Thank you."

Austin kissed me again and I smiled against his lips. "We're getting sidetracked."

He nodded. "I like getting sidetracked with you."

I blushed again.

"Anyway, I'm a genius," he said.

"Huh?" I choked on my sip of wine and coughed to clear my throat. Austin rubbed my back until I was able to catch my breath. "That's the last thing I thought I'd hear out of your mouth."

He chuckled. "Picked up on that."

"Are you really a genius?"

"I'm really a genius. My IQ's one-seventy-one."

"Shut up." I stared at him for a second, hoping to see if he might flinch revealing a lie. He didn't. "If you're a genius, how is it you're a part of a gang?"

He raised an eyebrow. "A gang?"

"*Please,* I will admit that I'm somewhat sheltered, but I know enough to know that motorcycle clubs are pretty much glorified gangs, Austin."

He laughed. "Fuck me, you're adorable."

I shoved at his shoulder and slid off his lap, rising to my feet.

"What did I say?" he asked.

"Nothing."

"Babe. I don't play that game. Somethin' crawled up your ass. Tell me what it was."

"If you must know, you hit a nerve," I snapped.

"No shit." He leaned forward, settling his arms on his knees. "How'd I do that?"

I bit my lip and set my wine on one of the side tables. I took a minute to study him and then I decided if he wanted to get to know me, he was gonna get to frickin' know me.

I knew when he did, he'd run as far as he could and never look back. "I'm the baby of the family. I was what could only be described as a surprise. Elliot was ten when my mom found herself pregnant with me, Emily was twelve. They thought they were done."

"Okay," he said.

"I have always been 'adorable' and 'cute' and 'naïve,'" I used air quotes after each description, "and until a few years ago, I was even 'lucky' enough to be a virgin. Because my sister is an ADA, my brother is a detective, and my father is the chief of police, I have always lived in a bubble of over-protectiveness. If I liked a guy and he liked me back, either my brother threatened death if he touched me, or it would never get past a kiss when they found out who they'd be up against." I took a deep breath. "And you know what? They were right, because the one guy who pushed past them is the one who stole all my money! I have worked really hard to forget about all of that, but when you speak to me like I'm nothing more than a cute face, it hits a nerve and reminds me just how incredibly stupid I am."

"Let me make sure I'm hearing you." Austin stood and closed the distance between us. "Because I think you're beautiful and sexy as hell, that led us to you feeling stupid?"

I snorted. "I'm not sexy."

"Babe." He frowned. "You are."

"I'm fat."

"Fuck me, you are *not*." He scowled. "You've got a real body, babe. Not a runway model, eat a fuckin' sandwich, kind of boney ass one. And by the way, most men like something soft to hold onto. I do."

"Austin," I admonished, and looked at my feet. "Stop it."

"Hey." He slid his hand to my neck, his thumb stroking my pulse before lifting my chin. "I get that that asshole did a number on you, and I plan to deal with that, but you need to know something. I don't lie. So, when I say you're adorable, it means you're fucking adorable, but it also means I think you're funny and, from what I've seen so far, quick. Shit, baby, your observations and sense of humor are not those of someone stupid. Then, pile on the fact I want to fuck you… that means you're sexy as hell."

I couldn't breathe. No one had ever made me feel the way he did and I'd known him for a little over twenty-four hours. "Wow," I rasped. He grinned, leaning down to kiss me, but I laid my fingers over his mouth before he reached me. "What did you mean by you were going to deal with that?"

"See?" he said against my hand. "Quick."

I lowered my hand and leaned back to meet his eyes. "Are you going to tell me?"

"I'm not."

"Seriously?"

He cocked his head. "I thought you wanted to know about my genius status and why I joined my 'gang.'"

"First, why do you wear a vest *and* a jacket?"

"This is a cut, babe. It tells the world who I am. The jacket's for warmth or for when I ride."

I bit the inside of my cheek. "I sound stupid when I ask these questions, don't I?"

He frowned. "Not at all. You sound curious. I love that you want to know about me."

I smiled. I liked that answer. "Okay, you can tell me about your genius status now."

Austin chuckled and tugged me back to the sofa, pulling me down beside him. He wrapped an arm around my waist and pulled me back against his chest as he leaned back and settled his feet on the coffee table again. I liked this position almost as much as I did his lap. Almost.

"I have the typical rough childhood sob story," he began. "Mom died of an OD when I was six, Dad was an abusive alcoholic, so me and my sister came to live with an aunt out here…"

"Where are you from?"

"Originally? Tennessee."

I smiled. "I thought I detected a southern accent."

"Yeah, I'm surprised I haven't lost it considering how long I've been here," he said.

"I like it. It's kind of sexy."

He grinned. "Not stupid, baby. Take that in, yeah?"

"I'm not stupid because I think you're sexy?"

"Damn straight."

"Good to know," I said. "So, what happened after you went to live with your aunt?"

"All hell broke loose. My aunt was a bitch and she broke my sister's arm, so we were put into the system."

I craned my neck to look up at him again. "You have a sister?"

He nodded. "She's two years younger than me."

"Did you stay together?"

"No. She was sent to live with a couple who adopted her. They felt I was a bad influence, so they wouldn't let her see me."

"They did?" I linked my fingers with his and squeezed his hand. "Austin, I'm so sorry."

"Not your fault, baby," he said.

"I know, but still, that must have been really hard."

"Not gonna lie. It sucked."

I looked up at him and smiled. "I bet it did."

He kissed me quickly and then pulled me close again. "Over the next ten years or so, I was shuffled around from one shithole to another and then when I was eighteen, I aged out."

"That's awful."

He shrugged. "It is what it is."

"Where's your sister now?"

"She married a doctor I think."

"You don't keep in touch?" I asked.

"No."

"I'm sorry," I whispered.

He kissed my temple and gave me another gentle squeeze. "When I was nineteen, my foster sister Annie called me... she'd been in the last place before I aged out and she was in trouble. She was drunk and some guy was smackin' her around, so I got her out and took her home. What I found out later was that our foster father had been molesting her and child protective services did nothing about it."

I gasped and turned to face him. "What do you mean? Did she report it?"

Austin nodded.

"Officially?" I pressed.

"Yeah, babe. Officially. They buried it." He frowned. "Or they tried to. I found it."

"You found it? How?"

He scowled. "I hacked into their system and found the report. It landed me in jail."

I gasped again. "You went to jail because you hacked CPS's system?"

"No, I went to jail because I beat the shit out of our foster dad. Put him in the hospital and wasn't street smart enough yet not to get caught. Jail is where I met Crow and he's the one who gave me a purpose."

"Crow?"

"He's our Prez."

I shook my head. "I'm assuming that's not his real name?"

"It's his legal name. Crow Butler."

"Shut up."

He grinned.

"So, Crow gave you purpose. How?"

"He bailed me out, gave me a family," he said. "Became the father I never had. I owe him everything. And he needed a little help protecting the club from an ex-member who had computer skills as good as mine. Better, even. But in answer to your original question, I don't speak like a thug because I have to work with highly educated people on a regular basis, so Crow made sure that I could converse with them properly. I'm "Booker" because, not only did I used to have my nose in a book most of the time, I do the club's books."

"Wow." I dragged my legs in front of me, criss-cross style, and leaned forward to study him. "What happened to your foster dad?"

"He was arrested once the evidence was released and several other girls came forward. He was an asshole, but I could deal with that, I was sixteen when I went to live with him, and other than verbal abuse, he never touched me. He probably knew I'd kill him if he did. But I wish I'd known about Annie before I left. I could have protected her."

"Where is she now?"

"She's an old lady to one of our California charter's members. She's protected."

I settled my chin in my hand. "How does the old lady thing work?"

"Lookin' to be one?"

"Ah, no, I don't think so." I wrinkled my nose and sat up a bit. "It's a horrible title."

Austin dropped his head back and laughed. "It's a title of honor, babe."

"How is calling a woman 'old' a title of honor?"

He tugged on my hand, lifting it to his mouth and kissing my palm. "It just is."

I shrugged. "If you say so."

He released my hand and pulled his cell phone from his pocket. "Yo," he said as he answered it.

So much for my "doesn't talk like a thug" theory.

"Yeah I'm here." Austin glanced at me and then

frowned. "Shit, are you serious? Tell the little fucker it's not gonna happen. No, Mack, it's not a fuckin' option." He rose to his feet and stepped outside. I was left sitting on my couch in the same position I'd been in for the last fifteen minutes and wondering what the heck was going on.

FIVE

Danielle

I UNWOUND MYSELF from my seat and made my way to the kitchen. I was starving, but hadn't made it to the store due to my lack of a car situation, so I didn't have much in the way of food. It was just past six, so ordering a pizza was probably my best option. More of a hit to my bottom line, but now that the pressure was off with the car repairs, I figured I could splurge a little. Don't get me wrong, I fully intended to pay Austin back; I just had to save a little first.

Grabbing my laptop, I powered it up and pulled up the pizza delivery menu. Two pizzas for under fifteen bucks suited me perfectly and the leftovers would last a while, but before I could hit the order key, Austin walked back in.

"Everything okay?" I asked.

He nodded. "Club business."

"Which means, it's none of mine, right?"

"I'm starving," he said without acknowledging my question. "You hungry?"

"I was just going to order pizza." I focused back on the screen. "My cupboards are bare, I'm afraid, so I've got nothing to cook." I glanced up at him. "Do you want to stay?"

He chuckled. "Did you think I was leaving?"

I shrugged. "You didn't say either way, so I'm flying blind here."

He sat next to me on the sofa again. "Pepperoni would be good."

"Okey dokey." I put the order in and then set my computer on the coffee table. "Want another beer?"

"In a minute." He pulled me onto his lap again and kissed me.

I was so unprepared for his ability to throw me around like I weighed next to nothing; I had to grab his shoulders to keep from falling off of him. He shifted me under him, stretching out beside me never once releasing my mouth as he stroked my neck, moving his hand to cup my bottom.

I felt my nipples tighten and my breasts grow heavy with desire as he deepened his kiss. What he could do with his mouth was surely illegal somewhere in the world and I found myself weaving my fingers into his hair. Crap... even his hair was sexy.

Austin broke the kiss and dropped his forehead to mine. "Fuck me, you can kiss."

I licked my lips and took a deep breath. "Back atya."

He rubbed his nose against mine and smiled. "I had planned to take this a lot slower."

"Well, I hadn't planned you'd take it anywhere at all,

so I guess that makes us kind of even."

"We're gonna make this work, babe. You'll see."

"You don't even know me," I argued. "You seem awfully sure."

"When I see something I want, I don't hesitate to make it mine, Dani." He ran his finger across my collarbone. "It's good you get that now. It'll cut down on any confusion later."

"So you've seen me, you want me, and I'm to be another conquest?" I challenged, pushing at his shoulders.

"I don't do conquests, babe." Austin smiled, holding me tighter and leaning down to kiss my nose. "But I will do you."

"Charming," I ground out.

"Don't typically do flowers, babe, but tell me your favorites and I'll buy 'em for you."

"Don't bother." I pushed at his shoulders again, but he didn't move.

My doorbell rang and it was the perfect opportunity to put distance between us, but apparently, Austin wasn't done and he kissed me again.

"The pizza's here," I said as the doorbell pealed again.

He nodded. "We're gonna eat, then we're gonna talk some more."

"I think you've said enough."

"Babe," he said with a sigh.

"Let me up so I can pay for the pizza."

"You're not payin' for the pizza, Dani."

I let out a frustrated groan. "You are *not* the boss of me."

He climbed off me. "For the sake of our current argument, baby, let's say I am."

I couldn't stop my jaw from dropping open as he sauntered away from me toward my front door. I knifed off the sofa and made my way to the kitchen muttering to myself. How could a man who drove me so frickin' crazy manage to also make me mad with desire? It didn't make any sense to me.

Austin joined me, setting the food on the counter as I opened the fridge, but before I could grab him another beer, he wrapped an arm around me and turned me to face him. His hand went to my neck again, his thumb to my pulse, and he studied me for several seconds. "I wasn't expecting you."

I sighed. "Same."

"Will you be patient with me, Dani?"

I shook my head. "We can't do this."

"Yes, we can."

"We *can't*." I pulled away from him. "My family's all about the law, Austin. Your club's not. It's a total conflict of interest."

He leaned against the counter and crossed his arms. "My club's clean."

"Clean, clean, or just untouchable?"

He frowned.

"Club business?" I snapped.

"What the hell do you want me to say, Dani?"

"I want you to tell me something, anything. But I want the truth."

"Babe."

"Forget it," I said.

"Don't shut down on me, Dani. Just tell me what you're thinkin'."

"I just want you to be realistic. It's obvious we're attracted to each other, but you can't base a relationship on just lust."

"We're in a relationship now?" he challenged.

"Absolutely not." I took a deep, steadying breath. "How about you take your pizza and go? I'll find a way to pay you back for the car. I really appreciate all your help." I started for the front door. "I hope you have a nice life."

I'd made it just past my dining table when he grabbed

my arm and tugged me into his arms. His mouth slammed onto mine and he kissed me with an intensity I'd never experienced before. I hated that I loved it. Hated that I couldn't resist him. Hated that heat pooled between my legs as he slid his hand under my shirt.

Austin broke the kiss with a scowl. "You're a fuckin' pain in my ass, baby."

"Then leave."

He shook his head. "Not gonna happen."

"I don't understand what you want from me," I snapped.

"I'm gonna show you."

I shook my head. "Not tonight you're not."

"Dani," he said, his tone pitched low in warning.

"What, Austin?" I bellowed. "I don't know you. I'm not jumping into bed with you just because I'm attracted to you. For all I know, I could be one in a long line of women you like to "do" on a regular basis. I've heard about your types of gangs and how you pass women around and that is *not* me. You may be used to biker whores who like that... hell, they probably live for the chance to provide you with fellatio... or other kinds of sexual favors, but I'm not one of them."

"Fuck me." He raised an eyebrow. "Fellatio?"

"Yes. Oral sex."

"You think I'm standing here expecting you to suck me off?" he asked.

"Don't be crude," I said, my face on fire.

"You can't say it, can you, Dani?"

"I just did," I countered.

His hand went to my neck again, the familiarity of his thumb sweeping over my pulse, and he smiled. "Baby, one day... *soon*... you and I are gonna take this further. Maybe you'll suck my cock, maybe you won't, but I will definitely eat your pussy, and you'll love it. You will scream for more and I will oblige. I will take my time and make you come… more than once. I'm thorough and I'm very good at what I do, so you'll beg for more and when you do, I'll give you more." He stroked my pulse again. "What I will not do is share. Neither will you. Get me?"

I swallowed, squeezing my legs shut in an effort to stop my body's traitorous reaction.

"Dani?"

"What?" I rasped.

"Do. You. Get. Me?" he repeated.

I licked my lips and nodded.

"Good." He smiled again. "Let's eat."

I swallowed, but continued to stand where I was.

"Babe?" he said. "Food."

I nodded again and followed him back into the kitchen, wholly unclear on what had just happened. Austin seemed perfectly at ease, while I felt like I needed a cold shower.

We sat at my small dining room table and ate in virtual silence, Austin leaving me to my thoughts which really wasn't a good idea on his part, because I spiraled. Big time.

I made it through one piece of pizza before I realized if I ate another, I'd throw up. I took my plate back to the kitchen. Rinsed it, put it in the dishwasher, and turned to get his, but he was already right behind me.

His arms came around me and he gave me a squeeze. "You're gonna be fine, Dani. We're gonna make this work and you'll learn to trust me."

I did a face plant into his chest, wrapping my arms around his waist and breathing him in. He smelled delicious. Leather and cologne… not too heavy… but just enough to make me want to lick every part of his body, starting with his mouth. I shook off my thoughts and let him hold me. "You freak me out."

He chuckled. "I'm pickin' up on that."

I leaned back so I could see his face. "I feel like I've known you forever and that scares me. I just can't trust you this fast. It's unwise."

"I'm gonna give you time. You'll see."

"What do we do about my family?"

He shrugged. "Whatever you want to do. But if this works out the way I want it to work out, I'm gonna have to meet them."

I pulled away from him and poured a glass of wine. He leaned against the counter and crossed his arms while I sipped and contemplated. He let me think for about six minutes before he took the glass from my hand and put it on the counter. "I'm still working on that," I complained.

He pinned me in, his hands on either side of my hips, leaning against the counter. "You can have your wine in a minute. Right now, you need to listen to me."

I wrinkled my nose. "*Not* the boss of me."

He chuckled. "If you want me to be patient and wait, baby, you need to stop being cute."

"I'm not trying to be cute, I'm being serious."

Austin leaned closer. "That's why it's cute."

He kissed me, and damn it if I didn't melt right then and there. I had to figure out a way to get myself together and quit doing this. Of course, I thought of this while I slid my hands into his hair and deepened the kiss. Austin lifted me onto the counter and I wrapped my legs around him as he moved into me. His lips moved to my neck, while a hand went under my shirt and pulled one bra cup down, scraping a nail across my nipple. I gasped as he rolled it between his fingers and I couldn't help myself from pushing into his touch.

"Austin?"

"Mmm?"

"We need to stop," I said, my breath coming in short bursts.

"Fuck." He dropped his hand, lowered my shirt, and nodded.

I cupped his face and grimaced. "Sorry."

"I get it, babe. It's just gonna take me a minute."

Austin got himself together and then lifted me off the counter. I couldn't seem to stop yawning, but didn't want the night to end, so covered it as best I could.

"I should go," he said. "You're exhausted."

"I was hoping I could hide that better."

He stroked my cheek. "I'll take you to dinner tomorrow night."

I grinned. "Okay."

"Plan on Saturday nights to be our thing, yeah?"

"That all sounds amazing, but next week's out."

"Why?"

"Girls' night with Kim."

Austin frowned. "Blow her off."

"Um, no way. I only get one Saturday every other month when she blows off working at her very lucrative bartending gig to spend more than an hour here and there with me."

He shook his head. "Babe, I can't see you over the next few Sundays. I might be able to break away for a bit on Wednesday, but if I can't, I'm not waitin' an entire week to see you."

I grimaced.

"What?"

"I can't do Sundays either."

"Why the hell not?"

"It's dinner at my parents' place." I bit my lip. "It's a standing date for all of us every week."

"Shit!" He dragged his hands over his face. "Work with me here, Dani."

I chuckled. "Austin."

He cocked his head. "You think this is funny?"

I bit my lip and shook my head, but couldn't hold back a snort at his expression of incredulity. "Okay, it's a little bit funny."

He smiled slowly and I realized I'd possibly pushed

him a little further than I was prepared for. I backed out of the kitchen, him stalking me. I turned and made a run for my bedroom, attempting to close the door before he reached me, but failing miserably.

He bent at the waist and gently shoved his shoulder into my middle, tackling me onto the bed, and tickling me until I was sure I would pee. "Stop," I squealed.

"You gonna make it up to me?" he asked.

"How exactly am I supposed to do that?"

He kissed my neck. "I can think of a few ways," he whispered.

I had no idea what the hell was wrong with me, but this struck me as funny and I chortled, trying to squirm away from him as he gripped my hips and held me to the bed.

"That's funny to you?" he asked.

I pressed my lips into a thin line and shook my head, but it was useless, I couldn't stop giggling. Chalk it up to my lack of sleep, but I totally lost it. What I wasn't entirely expecting was him to laugh as well. He didn't stop tickling me, but he did laugh while he was doing it.

"Stop, stop," I said, breathless. "I'm going to pee."

He kept going.

"Stop, honey. Please."

He did. Immediately. "What did you say?"

"Stop, I'm going to pee?"

Austin shook his head. "No after that."

"Please?"

He squeezed my sides again and I squeaked in surprise, giggling again. I bit my lip and reached up to stroke his cheek. "Honey," I whispered.

"Fuck," he rasped, leaning down to kiss me. "I love that."

"You do?"

"Yeah, baby. I do." He rolled onto his back and groaned. "I need to go. If I don't, I won't."

I slid off the bed. "I'm free on Monday."

"Can't do Monday, baby."

"Okay. Well, I'm sure we'll find another night that works."

He nodded. "I'm gonna go now."

"Okay."

He rose to his feet and kissed me again before heading back out to the living room and grabbing his leather jacket. I felt somewhat dejected that he was leaving, but I knew that if he stayed, we'd go further than I was ready to, and lucky for me, he seemed to understand that. I don't know what it was about him, but I was falling fast, and that was new to me. I couldn't quite decide if I liked the feeling or not, but when he smiled his sexy smile and leaned down to kiss me again, I decided I didn't really care. He was delicious.

"Talk to you tomorrow," he said.

I nodded and pulled open the door again, but when he made to walk out, I grabbed his hand. "One more kiss?"

He grinned and left me with a kiss that made me want more as I closed the door and leaned against it. There was no way in hell I was going to manage sleeping when all I wanted was him to keep me occupied for the night. I forced myself not to call him back inside and headed to bed, my overwhelming exhaustion replaced with a kind of desire that no one but Austin "Booker" Carver would be able to satisfy.

I was in big, big trouble.

SIX

Danielle

SATURDAY NIGHT, AUSTIN arrived just before six and settled himself on my sofa. Although my makeup was applied, my hair was still in a towel, I was in a robe, and I had no idea what I was going to wear. We'd talked for less than five minutes during the day and he hadn't given me any details of the date.

"You haven't told me what we're doing."

"Get together at the club," he said.

"I thought we were going to dinner."

He smiled up at me from his position on the couch. "We are. Club's grillin'."

"So, we're not actually going out?" I frowned. "Like on a real date?"

"It's a real date, baby. And we're leaving your apartment, so it's 'out.'"

"What am I supposed to wear?" I asked.

Austin gave me a lascivious grin. "Jeans, tighter the better, low-cut top... somethin' like that."

"I don't own anything biker slut, Austin."

He shrugged and studied me. "Babe, it's family. Wear whatever the fuck you wanna wear."

"Well, that's so freaking helpful, *honey*. Thanks."

I stomped back to my room and into my closet. In the last thirty seconds or so, Austin had informed me that I'd be meeting his "family." He'd also not denied my need to wear something slutty. I didn't own anything slutty. I could maybe wear something a little low-cut, or wear one of the two little black dresses I owned, but he was in his "uniform" of jeans, tee, and cut, so I'd be way overdressed if I did.

I should probably bow out. If it was at the club, then it was probably going to be filled with criminals, and that would look really bad for my family. I sat on the floor of my closet and dropped my face in my hands. God, I was such an idiot. Why the hell did I even entertain the thought that this could work out?

"Dani," Austin said with a sigh.

I glanced up at him standing in the doorway. "What?"

"You're way overthinking this."

"I can't go with you tonight, Austin. I think it would be best for you to go alone."

He hunkered down beside me and smiled. "No."

"I think it's too soon."

"For what?"

"For me to meet your club." I frowned. "I hardly know you."

"Babe, it's a casual get together. No pressure."

"And just how many women have you taken to meet your club?" I asked.

"You're jealous?"

"No," I snapped. "I'm just wondering if we should wait to see if this goes anywhere before we start dragging our friends and family into it."

"Stop fuckin' around, Dani, and get dressed."

"No." I rose to my feet. "I'm not going."

"Yeah, you are."

"No, I'm not. It's a bad idea and you know it."

"How's it a bad idea?" he demanded.

"You're going to bring a kindergarten teacher who happens to be the daughter of a cop to a place filled with criminals! They're going to see me coming from a mile away and they will hate me just because I'm not like you."

His eyes widened. "Well, fuck me, baby. Thanks for puttin' words in their mouths and judging them before they can judge you."

"You're welcome," I retorted, and moved past him, but he caught my arm.

"Dani, the club's clean and no one'll hate you."

"You can't know that."

He smiled. "Babe, I *can* know that. We're not one per-centers."

"I don't even know what that means."

"I'll explain it to you one day. I promise."

"I'm not good with crowds," I confessed.

Austin gave me a sexy grin. "We can go to my room anytime you want to. Just say the word."

"You live there?"

"No. But I have a room there should I need it."

"See? I don't even know where you live," I said.

"I'll take you home sometime, baby. We're gettin' to know each other. It'll happen." He cupped my neck and thumbed my pulse. "What's really goin' on inside your head, Dani?"

"It's just that I know nothing about you and you're taking me to a place with people who know everything about you and with whom I have nothing in common. What will I talk about?"

"Whatever the fuck you wanna talk about."

"Well, that's helpful. Thank you."

"Babe. Get dressed. It's gonna be fine."

I drew my eyebrows together. "What if I follow you?"

"What?"

I bit my lip. "I'll follow you to the party. That way, you can stay if you want to, but I can leave if it's too much."

"Hell no."

"Why not?"

"My woman is not driving herself to a fuckin' family get together, Dani. That's why."

"I'm *not* your woman!" I pointed out.

"What the fuck?"

"We've known each other for less than a week," I continued. "I'm not your woman. We're not anything yet."

His mouth landed on mine with an intensity I wasn't prepared for. He tugged the towel from my head and slid open my robe, cupping my breast and rolling my nipple between his fingers. Guiding me to the bed, he pushed me down, placing one hand on my chest to keep me planted where he wanted me, while his mouth moved from my lips to my neck.

"Austin?" I rasped.

He didn't reply as he drew a nipple into his mouth and bit gently. I gasped at the sensation. Austin pushed open my knees, sliding my thighs over his shoulders and began a delicious assault on my clit. I whimpered as he sucked, licked, and kissed his way around my most private area.

He slid one finger inside of me, and then two, and as much as I tried to resist the fire burning inside of me, it was useless. I cried out as my orgasm hit and he kissed my inner thighs before releasing my shaking legs and climbing back up my body. "You are absolutely my fuckin' woman, Dani. Got me?"

I squeezed my eyes shut.

"Dani," he pressed. "Do you get me?"

"No, Austin, I don't," I admitted as I pulled my robe closed again and sat up. "You confuse me."

He leaned up on his elbow and raised an eyebrow. "How so?"

"Like you care," I ground out.

"Oh, I do care, baby," he droned. "Please tell me all the ways I confuse you so that I can clarify things for you."

"Screw you, Austin."

He laughed and sat up. "I was just tryin' to do that, baby. You stopped it."

"You are such a jerk!"

"I'm not tryin' to be, Dani." He dragged his hands down his face. "Tell me what's on your mind."

I sighed. "You're everything my parents warned me against. You're secretive, but you're also honest. I feel wholly protected by you, but then you scare me more than anyone I've ever known. You're a bad boy, but when I dated a so-called good one, he turned out to be the devil, so, yeah, I don't get you because you're not what I expected. You drive me crazier than anyone I've ever met, but then you make me feel complete. I'm feeling things I don't quite know how to process and that makes me want to run. I don't want to give up something that might be really, really good, but I also don't want to be stupid and fall for a boy just because he's super pretty and makes me come."

He shrugged, his nonchalance back in place. "I did tell you I would."

"You also promised you'd do it more than once."

"Happy to oblige, baby."

I tied my robe with an angry swoosh. "I'm pouring my heart out to you and you're talking about making me come again?"

He sighed and dragged his hands down his face. "Dani."

"What, Austin? I don't know what kinds of women you've dated in the past, but I'm not one who can be manipulated with your ability to be really good at oral sex, or kissing, or... well, anything oral," I said, lamely. "I deserve to be treated with respect and if you're not willing to do that, then see you later."

"Pain in my ass," he grumbled.

"Then *leave!*" I stepped into the bathroom and slammed the door.

My tirade had completely counteracted my body's sated state just moments before and that made me mad. I wanted to go back to my post-climax glow. I stared in the mirror and scowled at myself. I shouldn't look this way. My eyes were bright, my skin was flushed, and I looked more alive than I had in a long time. Despite my tirade, I felt happy. Austin did that for me. I knew that I could be totally honest with him. Show him one hundred percent of myself, even if it wasn't pretty. The door opened and I caught Austin's eye in the mirror. "I thought you were leaving."

He wrapped his arms around me from behind, pulled my hair to the side, and kissed my neck. "You show me that and expect me to leave?" he challenged.

"Yeah, kinda. It's been three days and I'm showing you everything." I sighed. "So much for wanting to be sexy and mysterious."

He turned me to face him. "You couldn't be more beautiful to me, Dani."

"I think there's something psychologically wrong with you."

"You could be onto something." Austin chuckled. "Meeting my brothers is a big deal, baby, but I've been trying to downplay it, so you don't panic on me."

61

"Maybe it's too soon, then."

He shook his head, cupping my neck. "They need to know who you are to me."

"Who am I to you?"

"Everything, baby," he said. "Everything."

"How can you say that?" I asked. "It's been less than a week."

Austin smiled. "You're what I want, Dani."

"Well that explains *everything*."

"You want out at any point in the night, you tell me. I'll take you wherever you want to go."

I fisted my hands in his shirt. "I want you glued to me all night."

Austin chuckled. "'Cause that's gonna be so hard for me."

I couldn't help but smile. "Okay."

"Okay?"

I nodded and he grinned before he kissed me.

"But," I continued. "I want to stop off at Freddie's and grab something to contribute."

"You don't need to do that, babe," he countered.

"I was raised that when you are invited to someone's party, home, get together, whatever, you bring something." I patted his chest. "So, we're going to bring something."

He shook his head. "Okay, baby, we'll stop."

"Thank you. Now, seriously. What should I wear?"

"Whatever you want, Dani."

"Jeans it is… but not as tight as you might require."

He laughed and patted my bottom. "Five minutes, baby."

"What? No! I can't dry my hair in five minutes."

"Then pull it back," he said.

"Hell, no," I snapped. "If I'm meeting your family, then I'm meeting them looking my best."

"Baby, you're gorgeous, doesn't matter what you

wear."

"Flattery will get you nowhere today, now go and let me do my thing."

"It gets me nowhere *every* day," he grumbled, and walked out the door.

I blow dried my hair with a stupid grin on my face, and the grin stayed put as Austin ushered me out the door forty minutes later and into his truck. I chose jeans, knee-high black leather boots, a black cardigan and red lace camisole. Casual, but still nice, and Austin's response after seeing me was to pull me in for another of his mind-blowing kisses, so I felt confident with what I was wearing.

After a quick stop at the supermarket for wine, beer, and a few snack items, we headed into Portland. Austin drove to another sketchy area in North Portland and I was glad we were in his truck. "Where are we?"

"Cully."

"Are all the businesses in bad areas of town?"

"The ones we don't want noticed are," he revealed, and reached over to link his fingers with mine. "I got you, baby."

"I know," I said quickly. "I've just never been here."

He chuckled. "That doesn't surprise me."

Austin pulled into the large lot of Big Ernie's Body Shop and parked. I couldn't help but wonder who Big Ernie was, considering he had two businesses named after him. Austin opened my door and helped me out of the truck before grabbing the bag of groceries from the back. I looped my purse over my shoulder, took Austin's free hand, and followed him through an unmarked door to the left of what looked like the actual shop.

A dimly lit hallway led to another unmarked door and Austin raised his face to the camera mounted on the ceiling and the door was pulled open. A small foyer with a few easy chairs and a desk with television sat in the space. A couple of bikers sat in the chairs, but they paused their conversation to eye me and Austin.

Austin released me long enough to greet the "brother" who'd granted entry. A man by the name of Cookie.

"Cookie, Dani," Austin said. "Dani, Cookie."

Cookie was older, probably in his fifties, tall with tattoos that covered his arms and went up his neck. He had patches on his cut as well, one of them read, "Vice President," so I assumed he was someone important. His dark hair was peppered with gray and he had a big bushy beard that worked very well for him.

I smiled and reached my hand out. "Nice to meet you."

He gave me a sexy grin and stared at my hand long enough for me to lower it and feel like an idiot. I moved closer to Austin, who wrapped an arm around me.

"You too, babe," he said, and turned toward the big room behind him. "Mags!"

"What?" A blonde woman with big hair and tiny clothes revealed herself from another doorway and walked over to him. Cookie pulled her into a passionate and borderline inappropriate grope session before grinning and facing us again.

"My old lady," Cookie said. "Mags, meet Booker's new woman. Dani."

Mags glanced at Austin and then me. "It's nice to meet you, honey," she said, her gravelly voice indication she probably smoked.

"We brought a few things," I said. "Where would you like them?"

She smiled. "What kinds of things?"

"Just some beer and wine, a few snack things and dessert."

"That was really nice of you." Mags raised an eyebrow at Cookie. "Wasn't that nice of Dani?"

"Yeah," Cookie said, slowly. "Real nice."

"Why don't you come with me, Dani?" Mags said, and took a second to kiss Austin on the cheek. "I'll show you where everything goes."

"Um... I..."

Austin handed Mags the grocery bag and beer, and leaned down to kiss me. "I'll find you in a minute."

I gave him a look I both hoped no one else saw, and that he took to heart. We'd been inside for barely a second and he was already ungluing himself from my side.

He chuckled and slid his hand to my neck. "One minute, baby."

I said nothing, considering it was either that or make a scene, and followed Mags through the door she'd entered from and into a large common room milling with people. The space was filled with sofas, overstuffed chairs, a pool table, large flat-screen television, several smaller tables that kids gathered around for board games, and three outdoor picnic tables.

Rough and ready looking men and women, all of whom you'd expect to see at a biker bar, laughed and drank, chased after kids, made out in the corner, or shot pool... all while smoking. The men wore jeans, boots, and cuts and the women wore a variety of biker chic attire, all of which were absolutely nothing like me or the people I hung out with. I felt like I'd been transported onto some form of a movie set full of extras.

I also couldn't have felt more out of place had I been abducted by aliens. Although, I did have a weird and ungracious thought that an alien spacecraft was probably cleaner and smelled better.

"Comin'?" Mags asked, already a few feet in front of me.

"Oh, yes. Sorry," I said, and rushed to catch up to her.

She led me into a commercial grade kitchen where another group of women were chugging beer and pulling out hamburger and hotdog buns, condiments, and bags of chips.

"Everyone, this is Dani," Mags said. "Booker's woman."

The group stopped what they were doing. And I mean, stopped. All of a sudden, I had ten sets of eyes on me, most curious, but one pissed. She was tall, probably five-foot-eight, dark hair with a purple strip dyed down the side and just as the rest of the ladies in the room, her hair was big. She wore a black pair of leather pants, a strapless bustier, and four-inch hooker boots. She looked like a porn star complete with fake eyelashes and even faker boobs.

I smiled, hoping it didn't look like a grimace. "Hi."

"It's nice to meet you. I'm Susie." A woman close to my height separated herself from the group and made her way to me. She was blonde like me, only not as natural as she might have been in her prime. She wore jeans, a low-cut T-shirt, and a vest that had "Property of Crow" on a patch. "I'm Crow's old lady."

"And my sister," Mags said.

I deduced Susie was the matriarch, because the rest of the ladies rallied around to introduce themselves to me, but not until Susie had led the way. Even the angry one pasted on a fake smile and introduced herself. Her name was Tiffany, but she told me to call her "Tiff." I tried not to throw up in my mouth.

"Dani brought a few things," Mags said, and lifted the bag onto the stainless-steel island.

"What can I do to help?" I asked, wondering where the hell Austin was.

Tiffany grinned at something or someone over my head and made a girlie saunter toward the door. I watched as she pulled Mack into an intimate embrace, her back to me, whispering something in his ear that had him rolling his eyes. He adjusted his expression before he smiled at her and then set her away and headed straight for me.

"Hey, Dani," he said sweetly, and kissed my cheek before looping a brotherly arm around my neck.

"Hi, Mack." I didn't miss the scowl and little stomp of

66

Tiffany's foot as she twirled and walked away.

"Did you meet everyone?" he asked.

"Yes. Thank you."

"Mind if I steal her?" Mack asked the other ladies.

"You kids have fun," Susie said. "Thanks for the stuff, Dani. Nice to meet you."

"You too." I let Mack lead me out of the kitchen and back into the great room. "Where's Austin?"

"He got caught up with something."

"How long will he be?" I asked.

"No idea, babe. Sorry."

I swallowed, my stomach churning with nerves. "Maybe I should go."

"I got ya, Dani. Come and meet a few of the brothers."

Mack grinned and I knew I didn't really have much of a choice, so I followed him around the room meeting the brothers and their women. I wasn't entirely sure I'd remember any of their names, but I tried to smile and not hide behind Mack as the men eyed me both curiously and suggestively. I recognized Hatch's name when Mack introduced me, and he put me at ease instantly. Long dark hair and a beard gave him a Rollo from Vikings look, and he had blue eyes that crinkled at the corners when he smiled.

I also knew I wouldn't forget Knight. He didn't stay long, but he made a lasting impression. I should figure out a way to introduce him to Kim. He was really tall, but so was she, so they'd be a gorgeous couple.

I was half an hour in, and still no sign of Austin, so I asked where the ladies' room was and got a chuckle from a few of the men.

"I'll show you," Mack said, and led me down another hallway and to the second door on the left. He banged on the door, got no response, so pushed it open, and indicated for me to enter.

"Thanks," I grumbled, and closed the door behind me.

Finding the light switch, I flipped it on and wrinkled my nose. *Gross.* A toilet, sink, and a white pressboard cabinet were all that sat in the relatively large space. It looked like a heavily used bar bathroom, complete with toilet seat up and empty toilet roll.

I opened the cabinet to see if I could locate more toilet paper and found a container of disinfectant wipes along with the warehouse rolls of paper, so I wiped the toilet down best I could before replacing the roll and doing my thing. After washing my hands and drying them with toilet paper... no paper towels anywhere to be found... I pulled out my phone and sent Austin a text.

I'm thinking I need to give you the definition of glued. You're obviously busy, so I'm going to call a cab.

I dropped the phone into my purse and pulled open the door, but it wasn't Mack on the other side of the door.

Austin grinned, sliding his hand to my neck and pulling me in for a kiss. "A cab, huh?"

"Where have you *been*?" I demanded.

"Sorry, baby, got caught up with the Prez. I'm all yours now. No more business."

I poked his side. "Jerk."

He laughed and lifted my hand to his lips. "Did you meet everyone?"

"I have no idea," I said. "Mack introduced me to a few people, but be warned, I won't remember who they are... except maybe Knight and Hatch. And I met Susie and a few of the other ladies when Mags took me back to the kitchen."

Austin nodded. "Those are the key women. They belong to someone."

"Belong to someone?"

He tugged me down the hall toward the great room. "Old ladies."

"Oh, right." I pulled him to a stop, and he faced me. "Who does *Tiff* belong to?" I asked.

"Fuck. She's here?"

I frowned up at him. "Yeah. She's here and really good at giving the stink eye."

"Ignore her. She's no one."

"She seemed pretty friendly with Mack."

"Mack's friendly with everyone." Austin cupped my cheek. "Hang in with me, yeah?"

"I feel totally out of place," I admitted. "Everyone's looking at me weird."

"What the hell? They're being rude?"

I shook my head. "No, they just keep looking at me like I'm an alien or something."

Austin laughed. "Babe."

"I'm the only one wearing clothes."

"I told you to wear what you feel comfortable in."

"I *am*," I stressed. "I just didn't realize I'd be wearing forty-two layers more than anyone else."

He grinned as he grabbed my hand and turned back toward the bathroom. "Come with me."

He led me past the bathroom, up a set of stairs, then another, down a wide hallway with doors every few feet, and into the last door on the left. Flipping on the light, he pulled me into his arms and kissed me. He slipped my purse from my shoulder and I let it fall as Austin guided me to a bed and laid me down on top of it, stretching out beside me. He continued to kiss me until I came to my senses and pulled away from him, flopping onto my back and taking several deep breaths.

Austin leaned over me and smiled, his hand settling in the middle of my chest. "You are the prettiest girl in the room, baby. That's probably why they're all looking at you. But no one will disrespect you, because they will answer to me, so you tell me if you run into a problem."

I stroked his cheek. "I'm a big girl, honey, I can deal. I just don't want to do this without you. I appreciate you sending Mack to help, but I don't want Mack. I want you."

He kissed me again, and then sat up and pulled me from the bed. "Glue."

"Yes, glue," I repeated. "If I have to put a leash on you, I will."

He wrapped his arms around me and slid his hands under my cami. "Don't make promises you're not willing to keep, baby."

I cocked my head. "Being leashed is a turn on for you?"

"If it means you're naked and I get more of what I did earlier, then fuck yeah."

Heat pooled between my legs. "You're killing me."

He straightened my shirt and cupped my cheeks. "Soon, baby. I'm not gonna be able to wait much longer."

"It'll be good for you," I quipped.

Austin groaned, but he did smile while he was doing it. "Leave your purse, babe. It'll be safe in here. I'm gonna take a leak."

While he headed through the door to the left of the bed, I took a minute to take in the room. The bed was nothing more than a mattress and box-spring on a low platform, but it was made, and the comforter and sheets looked clean. A very masculine gray, but clean.

A six-drawer black bureau sat against the wall, under the only window in the room, and a wooden door was partially open to reveal a closet with a few shirts hanging inside. If this was his room, he wasn't here often.

I heard the toilet flush and then the faucet turn on. Austin returned to the bedroom and smiled. "Ready?"

I grabbed my phone and slipped it into my pocket before taking his hand and following out of the bedroom. "How often do you stay here?" I asked.

"On average, about once a week."

"Where's your home?"

"I have a condo on Naito." He squeezed my hand. "I'll show you next week."

I grinned. "Sounds good."

We walked down the hallway, past the gross bathroom again, but before we reached the common room, Austin pulled us to a stop. "You good?"

"Glue, right?"

He smiled, leaning down to kiss me quickly. "Yeah, baby."

"Then I'm good."

The rest of the night flashed by so quickly, I wasn't entirely sure it had happened. I met everyone there, tried to remember everyone's names, but only managed a few. It helped that most of them had their names on their cuts. I got a lot less weird looks being in the presence of Austin, and I started to relax as the night went on. Could have been the wine as well, which was all I was drinking. I'd brought two bottles of my favorite red, and I was pretty sure I was the only one drinking it, as I never saw anyone else with anything other than beer in their hands.

I was leaning heavily against Austin, half listening to him talk to a couple of his brothers, my fourth glass of wine partially gone, when a little hand patted my thigh. I glanced down to see a little girl about four, her hair in a haphazard ponytail, her jeans on backwards, and her tiny little leather vest covering a pink shirt with roses on it. "Hi, wady."

I hunkered down beside her. "Well, hi. What's your name?"

"Lily."

"Hi, Lily. I'm Dani."

"My pants don't fit. Can you hewp me, pwease?"

I smiled. "They're just on backwards, honey. Where's your mom?"

"I don't have a mommy. My daddy's in his room."

I glanced up at Austin and raised an eyebrow. He shook his head and gave me an "I'll explain later" look. I took Lily's hand and rose to my feet. "How about we find somewhere a little more private to fix your jeans, hmm?" She gripped my hand and I handed Austin my wine as I narrowed my eyes at him. "Glue."

He smiled and gave me a chin lift in response.

I walked Lily to a little alcove behind the pool table where computers were set up along the window, and helped her with her tiny little motorcycle boots (seriously adorable) then I removed her jeans and helped her put them on the right way. "How did they get off you, baby?"

"I was going potty and I took them off," she said, as though it was obvious.

"Good job," I said. "Did you go potty by yourself?"

She nodded her head. "I can go like a big girl."

"I bet you can. But if you need to go potty again, how about you come find me if you can't find your daddy, okay?" I smiled. "That way we can make sure your jeans fit right."

I led her back out in the common area, just in time to see Tiff walking into the room, her body wrapped around a really good-looking man who looked to be in his early thirties. He was tall and lean, had dark blond hair, deep green eyes, and a handlebar moustache that covered full lips. I had never been one to find the meth dealer look appealing, but this biker rocked it.

"Daddy!" Lily squealed, and pulled away from me to make a run for him.

Tiff looked somewhat put out as the man caught his daughter, scooping her up in his arms and kissing her, but she schooled her features and made a good show of looking interested in the little girl.

"Where have you been, little girl?"

"The pwetty wady helped me," Lily squeaked, pointing at me.

The man followed her hand and raised an eyebrow at me. "Did she?"

"I had to go potty, Daddy, and I went all by myself,

72

but my pants didn't fit."

His eyes swept the room. "Where's Sally?"

"I don't know, daddy. She leff."

I heard the exchange as I made my way back to Austin. He slid his hand around my waist and kissed my temple. "That's Hawk," Austin whispered. "His old lady bailed on him three years ago, leaving him with Lily."

I frowned. "Seriously?"

He nodded and gave me a gentle squeeze. I focused back on the conversation, but found my hand gripped again by a familiar little one. I hunkered down beside Lily again. "Hi, honey."

"Hi, wady. I fugot you name."

I smiled. "Dani."

"Fank you for hepping me, Dani."

"You're welcome, honey."

"That goes for me, too," a deep voice said, and I looked up... way up, to see Hawk standing in front of me.

I stood and smiled. "No problem."

I was pulled tightly against Austin again and I had to grab his waist to keep from falling into him.

"Hawk," he said.

"Booker." Hawk gave him a chin lift and then turned to me again. "What's your name, babe?"

"She's with me," Booker said.

I reached out my hand. "I'm Dani."

"Dani." Hawk took my hand and gave me a sexy smile. "You're good with kids."

"Thanks. I love kids."

"What's your story?" he asked.

"I don't have a story." I smiled. "I'm pretty boring."

"I doubt that," he said, still holding my hand.

Austin stepped in front of me, effectively forcing me to step back.

Hawk dropped my hand and Austin scowled. "What are you doin', Hawk?"

"Just makin' conversation, Book."

"Fuck off."

"Austin," I hissed, glancing down at Lily. "Language."

"Yeah, *Austin*," Hawk droned with a shit-eating grin. "Watch your language."

"Daddy, can I have a cookie?" Lily asked, and Hawk scooped her up.

"What kind ya want?"

"Tocket Tip."

"One chocolate chip cookie comin' up," he said, and carried her toward the kitchen.

Austin grabbed my hand and tugged me away from the group, pulling me into the alcove I'd been in with Lily just minutes before. Pushing me against the wall, he covered my mouth with his and kissed me like his life depended on it. I kissed him back, but didn't let myself lose focus.

"Hey, what was that all about?" I asked after I broke the connection.

"Hawk can be an asshole."

"Okay. But he wasn't being one just then, honey."

"He was." Austin took a deep breath. "In his own way."

"There's obviously a story there."

He nodded. "Later."

"Are we going to hide here for a while?"

Austin chuckled. "I'd rather take you upstairs."

"Me too, honey... but it's not gonna happen tonight."

"Dani, Dani," Lily squealed as she rushed into the alcove, chocolate covering her face.

"Someone has a shadow," Austin grumbled.

I grinned and knelt in front of Lily. "How was your cookie?"

"I got you one."

"You did?"

She nodded and slipped her hand into her pocket, pulling out the crushed remnants of a cookie and holding out her palm. "Oops."

I laughed. "It's okay, baby. Let's get you cleaned up and find your dad, okay?"

"Glue, babe," Austin said as I stood.

I rose up on my tiptoes and kissed him quickly. "Glue, honey."

Walking Lily to the kitchen, I lifted her onto the counter next to the sink and turned on the water. The room was empty, so I found soap and paper towels in a cabinet above the sink. At least whoever stocked the kitchen had the forethought to keep things like this out of reach of little hands.

"Let's wash those hands." I helped her with the water and then wiped down her face, before setting her on the ground again. Her jeans would need to wait for the washing machine, but for now, she was good to go.

"You could have found me," a deep voice said.

I started a bit and turned to find Hawk lurking near me while I dried my hands. Lily had skipped off somewhere else, obviously perfectly comfortable in her own skin.

"She found me," I said, and smiled. "I didn't mind."

He crossed his arms. "She likes you. She doesn't typically like women. Used to men, 'suppose."

"You're raising a really sweet little girl."

"Seriously. What's your story, Dani?" he asked. "How'd you meet Booker?"

"I got lost and broke down outside the wrecking place. Aust—ah, Booker, came to my rescue."

"What do you do? You know, for a livin'."

"I teach kindergarten," I said.

Hawk dropped his head back and laughed. "You're shittin' me."

"Babe," Austin said from the threshold. "Ready to go?"

I nodded, dropped the paper towels I'd used to dry my hands in the garbage can next to the island, and skirted around Hawk to get to Austin. "Nice to meet you," I said.

"You too, babe," Hawk replied just as Austin grabbed me and kissed me a little too intimately before sweeping me out of the kitchen and back up to his room.

"Fuckin' asshole," he snapped, and slammed the door shut.

"Who?"

"Fuckin' Hawk."

"Okay, you need to tell me what's up with him. He was really nice to me, honey, and Lily's adorable."

"He wants you."

"What?" I squeaked.

Austin scowled. "He's got his fuckin' sights on you, which means I have to deal with his form of bullshit."

I don't know why, maybe it was the wine, but his little jealousy-induced hissy sent me into a giggling fit.

I quickly found myself lifted and dropped onto his bed, his hands at my waist. "You find this funny, huh?"

I tried to scooch away from him, nodding as I continued to laugh uncontrollably.

"Fuck, baby, you're gorgeous," he rasped as his hands left my waist and moved under my cami to cup a breast.

I arched into his hand as he pushed up my clothing, bra and all, and drew one nipple into his mouth, then the other. How he did it, I have no frickin' clue, but he removed the top half of my clothing faster than I was ready for. He tugged off his cut and shirt and then he was back to laving attention on my breasts again.

The feeling of his smooth chest against mine was delicious. I'd messed around with a couple of high school boyfriends a few times, but no one this muscular, and then there was Steven who was more fuzzy teddy bear than hot biker sex machine. God, Austin was irresistible.

He moved his mouth from my breasts to my lips as he unbuttoned and unzipped my jeans. His hand slid inside, under the band of my panties, and between my legs. I squirmed at his touch, his thumb sliding to my clit.

"Soaked," he whispered against my lips.

I nodded, my breath coming in short bursts.

He grinned and slipped two fingers inside of me. "Beautiful."

I stroked his cheek as he intensified the pressure. "Back atya."

I was just about to come when a banging at his door had him yanking his hand away from me and sitting up while I whimpered in frustration.

"What?" Austin demanded.

"Booker, Prez needs you," Mack called.

"Can it wait?" he bellowed.

"No."

"Fuck," he grumbled. "Gimme a minute," he called, climbing off the mattress and heading to his bathroom.

I covered my face with my hands while he washed up. The touch of his lips on my stomach had me cupping his face.

"I'm sorry, baby. Shit's happening right now."

"Can you call me a cab?" I asked, sitting up and searching for my clothes.

"Stay."

"No. I think I should go," I insisted. "We can't do this right now, honey. Not yet, anyway, and if I stay, it'll be too hard to stop."

He frowned. "I'll have Mack drive you home."

"Will he mind?"

He shook his head. "Give me a minute."

I nodded and he stepped out of his room as he pulled on his shirt. He peeked inside, made sure I was dressed, and pushed open the door. "Mack'll drive you."

"Okay, thanks."

He cupped my face and kissed me quickly. "Text me when you get home."

"Okay, honey."

He ushered me out of the room and into Mack's capable hands, and then went to do the Prez's bidding. Mack dropped me home, walked me to the door and checked my apartment for who knows what.

Once he was gone, I locked up, texted Austin, and poured myself a glass of wine. I was too wired (and horny) to sleep.

SEVEN

Danielle

"DANI?" EMILY REACHED over and squeezed my arm.

"Sorry, what?" I focused on her sitting next to me at the dinner table. I'd been distracted all evening, my date with Austin the night before swimming around my mind.

"What is going *on* with you?" she asked, grinning like she knew something I didn't.

My sister was not only highly intelligent, but also gorgeous, glamorous, and very, very taken. She was tall and blonde, with emerald green eyes, and a body to die for. She'd married Mitch Parsons right out of law school, and it was coincidentally their fifteenth wedding anniversary, which we were celebrating tonight. Mitch was also gorgeous, but in a rugged way. He'd been a cop before he changed careers and turned to bounty hunting. He loved my sister with an intensity that was sometimes scary, but she'd admitted it was also a huge turn on.

They had two gorgeous and glamorous children, Brandon, who was twelve-years-old, and Amelia, who was ten. They sat across from us, their blond hair perfectly coiffed, their behavior impeccable, and their senses of humor on overdrive. They were great kids and I adored them.

"Nothing," I said, quickly. "Just didn't sleep much last night."

Because Emily was so incredibly smart, she could see through me... truth be told, she could see through most people... with ease. She was often underestimated because she was so pretty, which she used to her advantage any time she could.

My sister raised an eyebrow. "Liar," she whispered. "Spill."

"*Em*," I hissed.

She leaned closer. "You've met a guy!"

I shook my head.

"What are you two conspiring about," our mother asked.

"I'm trying to get Dani to go out with a friend of mine," Emily improvised.

"And it's not going to happen," I said.

"Go easy on the baby, Em," Elliot piped in. "Her date the other night was a total bust."

"Was it?" my father asked. "That's a shame."

I choked on my wine as everyone laughed. "Say that a little more believably, Dad."

"I'm surprised you haven't forced her to wear a chastity belt," Emily said.

"I have always allowed you girls to make your own choices," he said.

"Ohmigod, Dad," I droned. "You are such a liar."

"Is that allowed in law enforcement?" Emily mused. "Lying to your children?"

"I think Ell should arrest him for being really bad at it," I said.

"Leave your father alone," my mom said. "He's very, very pretty... he can't be good at lying too."

That sent us all into fits again, including my niece and nephew.

"How about Dani and I do the dishes and get dessert ready?" Emily suggested. "Mom, you go relax for a bit."

Mom grinned. "I won't say no to that."

"Who wants to play pool?" My dad asked.

"Me!" Brandon said. "Can I, Mom?"

"You and your sister clear," Emily said. "And then you're free."

Mitch chuckled. "I'll help, then I'm gonna beat my kids' butts at pool."

"Not even gonna happen, Dad," Amelia droned.

"We'll see, honey."

She chuckled and started to clear the table.

Once Emily and I were blissfully alone in the kitchen, she scraped plates while I rinsed and loaded the dishwasher.

"Okay, girlie, spill," Emily demanded.

I sighed. "The guy that fixed my car is gorgeous and confusing and scary. And he's decided we're 'gonna get to know each other.'"

"Wow, all of that, huh?"

I nodded.

"Who is he?" she asked.

I bit my lip and dropped forks into the basket.

"Dani?"

"He's a biker, Em."

She cocked her head. "Like Tour de France?" she joked.

"Like Hells Angels."

Emily nearly dropped a plate into the garbage can. "He's in the Hells Angels?"

"No...Dogs of Fire." I faced her and grimaced. "Right? I can't do this."

"Why can't you do this?"

"Because all I keep coming back to is that all I know about motorcycle clubs is what I've seen on television, and that's pretty limited. I have no idea if he's a criminal or if he kills people. He says the club's clean, but I'm just not sure." I shook my head. "Even saying that out loud makes me sound like an idiot."

"It doesn't, honey," Emily assured me.

"He's gorgeous, Em, but he's also really bossy and I think he's used to having people do exactly what he tells them to do, because he gets all weird when I defy him. Like it's alien to him."

Emily laughed. "Welcome to the club, babe."

"Really?"

"Hells yes. Mitch is the same way. Well, he was."

"He was? But he's so sweet with you and the kids."

She smiled. "Yes, he is, but he's also bossy and protective, and if another man looks sideways at me, or disrespects me, he's pissy about it because he can't beat the shit out of him. Or at least, he doesn't do that anymore."

"He beat people up?"

"Oh, honey, yes. When we were first together, it was a huge problem because I couldn't just vent to him about the assholes I had to deal with. He'd actually go and have a "conversation" with them before I could work it out. He was constantly getting in my business and making things a lot harder for me. We had a come to Jesus meeting and when he still continued to do it, I dumped his ass."

I gasped. "You didn't."

"I totally did." She set a plate on the counter. "I needed him to understand that I was a grown ass woman and for the most part, could fight my own battles. I'm an officer of the law so to speak, I couldn't have my man breaking it in order to make my life easier. I still have to be careful sometimes with how much I tell him, which is hard, because he's my best friend, but he's also much better about letting me work stuff out myself."

"What if you can't work it out?"

Emily bit her lip. "Then I have asked him not to use his fists."

"Ohmigod, Em. Seriously?"

She nodded with a grin. "Sometimes it's nice to have a badass husband willing to defend your honor."

"I guess so."

Emily leaned against the counter. "Give me this guy's info and I'll run him through the system."

I sighed. "Kimmie said I should do that, too. Of course, she said I should make Elliot do it."

Emily rolled her eyes. "I wonder if there will ever be a woman able to resist him."

I shrugged. "Doubtful."

"We don't need to get the men involved," she said. "You and I can handle it on this end, I think."

I grinned. "You're the best sister ever."

"Back atya."

Family dinner wrapped up and after hugs all around, I headed home.

I arrived to find Austin waiting for me in the parking lot. He was standing next to one of the prettiest Harley-Davidsons I'd ever seen (limited exposure, of course, but it really was pretty) and he was dropping his phone into his jeans pocket as I stepped out of my car.

"Hi," I said.

He lifted his chin. "Hey, babe."

He closed the distance between us and leaned down to kiss me.

I smiled. "I thought you were busy tonight."

"Had a break. Wanted to see my girl."

This sent a thrill down my spine. "And who might that be?"

He chuckled. "How was dinner?"

"It was good," I said, and started up the stairs. "How long's your 'break'?"

"I've probably got about an hour."

"Want to come in for a drink or something?" I asked.

"Or somethin'."

I unlocked my door, leading him inside. I shrugged out of my coat and hung it up, while Austin dropped his onto a chair and planted himself on the sofa. I grabbed him a beer, poured myself a glass of wine, and sat beside him on the couch. In the light, I could see the stress on his face and frowned.

"You okay?" I asked.

"Shit day."

"Want to talk about it?"

He shook his head. "I can't, babe."

I sighed. "You look tired."

"I am." He took a sip of his beer.

"What time did you get to bed last night?"

"I didn't."

"Seriously?" I frowned. "Mack dropped me off at eleven. You didn't go home after the meeting?"

"Had a thing." He smiled tiredly. "Got about two hours of sleep this morning."

I set my wine on the coffee table. "Have you eaten?"

He checked his watch. "Not since this morning."

"Austin," I admonished, and rose to my feet. "I'm going to fix you something to eat at least."

His phone buzzed and he nodded. "Appreciate it, baby."

He answered his call and I headed back to the kitchen. I pulled out bread and cheese, figuring grilled cheese was quick and easy to prepare, and it would tide him over for a little while.

I was setting the food on the table when he walked back into my apartment, his face grim… well, grimmer than it had been twenty minutes ago.

"You okay?"

He nodded and sat at the table, devouring the food in record time. "Thanks, babe," he said, and dropped his plate into the sink.

"Got time to sleep for a bit?" I asked.

Austin shook his head, sliding his hand to my neck.

"What can I do?"

"You're doin' it, babe. You make everything better," he said, and pulled me close.

I wrapped my arms around his waist and squeezed. A familiar scent registered and I leaned back. "Why do you smell like gun powder? Please tell me you were at a firing range."

"Sure."

"Are you carrying?"

He stroked my cheek. "I'm always carrying."

"You're scaring me a little, honey. What's wrong?"

"Nothin' that won't be handled tonight, so I just have to deal."

"Are you in danger?"

"Not currently, no."

"That's not what I mean," I said.

"I know, baby, but I can't talk about it."

"Fine." I settled my cheek against his chest and closed my eyes. He stroked my hair and kissed the top of my head and we stood like this for a while. Our peace, however, was disturbed when he answered his phone again.

"Yo." He tried to pull away, but I held him tighter, so he settled and wrapped an arm around me. "Yeah. No. What do Crow and Hatch say? Shit. Yeah, I'm here. No. Okay. Fuck me, Mack. Yeah. Fine. Okay. If that's the case, then I'm gonna grab some shut-eye. See ya." He hung up and dropped his phone in his pocket again.

"Are you staying?" I asked.

He chuckled. "Kind of you to offer, baby."

I smiled up at him. "Well, you pretty much announced you were going to, so I have benevolently decided not to kick you out."

Austin laughed. "Appreciate that. I'll lock up and meet you in the bedroom."

"Um, *no*," I countered. "I'm going to bed. *You're* sleeping on the sofa."

"You're fuckin' hilarious, baby."

"I'm serious, Austin."

He frowned and shook his head. "Not sleeping on your fuckin' sofa, Dani. Also, not gonna fuck you if you don't want me to fuck you. What I *am* gonna do is hold my woman and sleep until I'm called up again."

"I am not a slut, Austin."

"Never said you were." He scowled down at me. "What the fuck, Dani?"

I bit my lip. "This is just going too fast."

"Jesus, Dani." He set me away from him and left the kitchen to lock up the apartment, returning quickly, and grabbing my hand. He led me back to my bedroom and faced me. "What side?"

"Excuse me?"

"What side of the bed do you want?"

I let out a frustrated sigh. "Window."

He laid his gun and phone on the nightstand by the door and promptly removed his clothes, graciously keeping his boxer briefs on. I swallowed at the sight of his body. God, it was still as magnificent as I remembered. He pulled the covers back and flopped onto the mattress, linking his hands behind his head. "You comin'?"

"I… um… have to take my makeup off and brush my teeth."

"Be quick, babe, yeah?"

"No funny business."

"I'm too tired for funny business."

I shook my head, my attempt at keeping him out of my bed a big fat failure, and headed to the bathroom. After removing my contacts, washing my face, and brushing my teeth, I opened my closet, found some pajama bottoms and a cami and changed into them in the closet. I flipped off the light and made my way to the bed, pulling the covers back and slipping inside. I was promptly pulled onto Austin's chest and kissed to distraction.

He rolled me so his chest was to my back. "'Night, baby."

"Goodnight," I whispered.

I scooted closer and his arms tightened around me. I smiled as I closed my eyes. This was pure bliss.

EIGHT

Danielle

I WAS AWOKEN Monday morning by my alarm. My bed was empty, but the delicious smell of Austin was still attached to my sheets.

I rubbed my eyes and stretched. I had parent-teacher conferences all day, so I needed to get my butt up and moving, but all I wanted to do was turn back time so I could snuggle up to Austin again.

"'Mornin', babe."

I turned my head toward the door to find Austin standing at the threshold. He wore jeans, sans shirt and he was positively edible.

"Mmm, hi." I sat up and smiled. "I thought you'd be gone by now."

"Didn't get called up." He stretched out on the bed and pulled me on top of him. "How'd you sleep?"

"Better than I ever have." I ran my fingers over his chest. "Why?"

He gave me a sexy smile and shrugged. "Nothing."

"Um, no. We don't play the nothing game, remember?"

Austin chuckled. "You talk in your sleep."

I sat up with a gasp. "I do not."

"You absolutely do."

"What did I say?"

He grinned and slid off the bed. "*That* I'm not gonna tell you."

"What? Why not?"

"Because I don't have to." He leaned down and kissed me. "Now, get ready for work and I'll drop you off."

"You have your bike."

"A recruit dropped off my truck."

"I'm fine to drive. Then I don't have to find a ride home."

"I'll pick you up when you're done."

I smiled. "I thought you were busy tonight."

"Plans changed."

"What if *I'm* busy?"

He grinned and kissed me again. "Are you busy?"

"No, damn it."

Austin laughed and grabbed his shirt off the floor. "Get ready, baby. I'll make coffee."

I made my way to the shower and got ready for work. When I ventured out of the bedroom, I found Austin had made me coffee, eggs, and toast. "Wow. Thank you."

"You're welcome." He grinned and kissed me.

I sat at the table and sipped the coffee. "You make a mean cup of coffee, Austin Carver."

"Good to know. Barista will be a good option should I

need a second job." He sat beside me and watched me eat. "What time you done today?"

"My last conference is at two-forty-five, so I'm guessing around three thirty. Sometimes we're done early, but I can text you when I know."

He nodded. "It stays nice, you're on my bike."

"No."

"What? Why not?"

"I can't." I set my mug down. "I… I'm terrified of motorcycles."

"You'll be fine."

"You're going to go all the way home to get your bike?"

"I'm going to be over that way, anyway."

I shivered. "I've never been on a bike, Austin. I'll make you crash."

He chuckled. "There is nothin' you could do to make me crash, baby."

I picked up my coffee again. "I'm sure I could think of a few things."

"Listen, there's nothing you could do outside of giving me head on my bike that would make me crash," he said. "And if you can figure out how to give me head while I'm riding, it'll be a fuckin' awesome way to go."

"Don't be gross," I ordered, my face on fire.

"Can't promise that."

"Why not?"

"Because you're gorgeous when you're caught off guard." He sipped his coffee again.

"You're an evil man." I wagged my finger toward him. "You know that, right?"

He leaned toward me and stroked my cheek. "I'm *your* man."

"You're my *evil* man."

Austin laughed and let me finish my breakfast.

* * *

I muddled through the day, my thoughts constantly turning to Austin and my total besotted-ness with him. I was never a fan of insta-love, particularly in romance novels, but now that I was living it, I was realizing how quickly I was falling for him.

My final parent was the single mom to Maverick, and he was one of my favorite kids, despite Austin's aversion to his name. His mom, Cassidy, was doing the best she could with limited resources, and I had nothing but respect for her.

She actually hung around and walked out with me once our conference ended. As we pushed open the double doors at the front of the school, she grabbed my arm and hummed in delight. I looked up to see Austin walking towards us.

"If I could have one night... just one... with a man who looked like that, I'd die happy," Cassidy mused. "I wonder who he belongs to."

I giggled. "That would be me."

"Shut the front door," she said. "Does he have any brothers?"

"Like a hundred," I retorted.

She pulled me to a stop. "Figure out a way to introduce me to them."

I laughed. "I'll invite you next time they have a get together."

"I'm gonna hold you to it."

Austin reached us, grinned, and leaned down to kiss me. PDA's were of no consequence to him it would seem. "Hey, babe."

"Hi." I grinned at Cassidy's expression. "Austin, this is Cassidy Dennis. Her son's in my class."

"Nice to meet you," Cassidy said, reaching out her

hand.

Austin shook it and smiled.

"I need to pick up Mav," she said, but continued to stare at Austin. "Ah, it was nice to meet you," she repeated.

"You too," Austin said, his expression one of amusement.

"'Bye, Dani."

"'Bye."

Cassidy walked off, glanced back a few times, but managed to climb into her car and drive off without running into anything.

"She wants to meet your club," I said.

"Excuse me?"

I nodded. "She saw you and nearly wet herself."

Austin laughed. "I take it she's a single mom?"

"She's the single mom of a darling little boy named Maverick."

"Fuck me," he said with a groan.

"Hmm-mmm," I droned. "Regret what you said?"

"Hell, no. That boy's gonna get his ass kicked in middle school."

"Not if he's a badass. Then it won't matter what his name is."

Austin chuckled. "You might have a point."

I ran my hand up his chest and stroked his neck. "Where's your truck?"

"Oh, my beautiful little temptress," he said, and kissed me quickly. "Your powers don't work on me when I have the chance to ride."

I wrinkled my nose. "Damn it! I was hoping it would rain."

"Come on, baby. You're gonna love it."

"But I have all my stuff." I lifted my bag and purse, filled with paperwork to finalize.

"Which will all fit perfectly in the saddlebags."

"I didn't bring a leather jacket. I don't even own one."

Austin grabbed my hand and grinned. "I brought one for you."

"You did not."

"I did, baby."

I had no choice but to follow him to his bike. It was just as pretty in the light of day, but that didn't mean it didn't scare me just as much. He took my bags from me and stowed them in his saddlebags once he'd pulled out a leather jacket that looked like it was made for me.

He helped me into it, handed me thick, leather gloves, and then helped me with my helmet. Everything fit perfectly. I'd had the forethought to wear my knee-high boots, but still I was shaking when Austin threw his leg over the bike. "Climb up behind me, Dani. Watch the pipes, they can get hot."

I craned my neck and asked, "How do I climb on?"

"Put your hand on my shoulder, foot on the peg, and throw your leg over."

"You make it sound so easy."

He grinned. "It is, baby. I've got the bike steady and I won't let you fall."

I licked my lips and did as he instructed. He held the bike, but looped his other hand to my waist when I climbed on to steady me. "You good?"

"No," I squeaked.

"Arms around my waist, baby, and scoot forward, tight to my back."

I followed his directions and felt a little more secure. He reached back and tugged on my thigh. "Pussy to my ass, babe."

"Gross, Austin." But I did slide further forward feeling even more secure.

"If you want to stop, yell or give me a squeeze, yeah?"

I nodded. "Okay."

He started the bike and pulled gently out of the parking

lot. I truly thought I was going to be sick, but once I got the feel of him and the bike, I began to relax. I'd ridden horses as a kid and found that if I moved with him, it was a familiar feel to riding. By the time we pulled off the freeway and onto Naito, I felt like a pro.

Austin pulled to a stop at a stoplight and grinned back at me. "You okay?"

"Yes."

"You sure?"

"This is frickin' fantastic," I yelled.

He laughed. "Want to keep going?"

I nodded.

"Okay, we'll go for a little ride, then."

When the light turned green, he veered down a side street and drove closer to the water. We couldn't go too far, but it was enough to put on a little speed before he pulled to a stop at a little lookout point. He guided the bike off the road and parked it, lowering the kickstand before turning off the engine. He twisted to smile at me. "You good?"

I nodded. "I think my legs are jelly, but that was amazing."

"You want to get off for a bit, or back to my place."

"Your place, I think. I'm a little cold."

"You got it, baby."

He started the bike again and I wrapped my arms around him tight as he pulled back onto the road and headed to his condo. He parked the bike, waited for me to climb off, despite my shaky legs, then he did the same and grabbed my things from his saddlebags. He helped me with my helmet and kissed me, the squeak of our leather jackets making me giggle. "I should tell my dad that the chastity belt is no longer necessary, considering leather has about the same effect."

Austin chuckled as he took my hand and walked me to the elevator bay, where we stepped into a car and rode to the tenth floor. He led me down the hall to a door directly at the end and unlocked it. Pushing it open, he stepped back for me to precede him inside.

I walked in and was assaulted by total, complete, and utter beauty. What Austin had failed to mention was his condo was in an exclusive building with an incredible view of the water. I gravitated toward the large picture windows that spanned his living room.

I didn't notice the hardwood floors, huge great room with fireplace, and open kitchen with granite countertops until way later in the evening. I was transfixed by the view of the water as the sun began to set.

Austin stood in front of me and unzipped my jacket, grinning as he removed it from my body as gently as he would a child. I couldn't stop looking at the way the clouds played off the water, and was amazed that boats would be out on such a chilly day.

My phone pealed in the quiet and I grabbed my purse and slid out my phone to answer it. "Hello?"

"Hey, hon," Emily said.

"Well, hi. How's my favorite sister?"

She chuckled. "Doing well. You got a minute?"

"Of course."

"Got info back on Austin."

I glanced at him in the kitchen pulling down cooking utensils. "What did you find?"

"He was arrested when he was nineteen."

"Yep." I nodded. "I know."

"Well, that's it, sis. Nothing else is flagging. He's a model citizen, doesn't even have a speeding ticket."

I don't know why, but this news relieved me. I didn't even realize I'd been concerned until now. "Awesome."

"Okay, gotta help Amelia with her homework. Love you."

"Love you too. 'Bye." I hung up and tapped the phone against my palm.

"Wine?" Austin asked.

I glanced at him and then back out at the water. "Yes, please."

I heard the pop of the cork and turned toward the sound, equally as impressed with his kitchen with top of the line stainless steel appliances. He'd removed his jacket and cut and stood in just a tight thermal shirt and his signature jeans. "Who was on the phone?"

"My sister."

"Everything okay?" he asked, and grabbed a glass from an upper cabinet, pouring my favorite wine into it.

I grimaced. "Full disclosure…she kind of did a background check on you."

He chuckled. "I'd have been disappointed if she didn't. I like that they watch out for you."

I grinned. "She only found your arrest."

He nodded. "Told ya, babe. The club's clean. Individually and collectively."

"Yes you did."

"Were you worried?"

"Not really," I said, and walked toward him. "But it's still nice to know my family isn't going to be."

He leaned down to kiss me quickly. "I've got you, baby."

"I know." I set my wine down. "Can I help?"

"Nah, I'm all set. Just make yourself at home."

"Are you always going to serve me like this?"

"Sure. We'll go with that."

I chuckled and walked back to the window. "This place is amazing."

"I like it."

"How long have you lived here?"

He scrubbed a couple of potatoes. "I bought it three years ago."

"You own it?" I asked, surprised.

He chuckled. "Yeah, babe. I own it."

"Sorry. I shouldn't sound so surprised."

Austin handed me the wine glass I'd left on the counter and then grabbed a beer for himself. He took my hand and led me to the huge sectional in the great room, pulling me down beside him. "I get why you're surprised, babe."

"You do?"

He nodded. "I have a pretty chaotic life, Dani, so when I come home, I want some form of order. I've always been like this. I like nice things and Annie helped me put a little bit of a feminine touch on it, mostly so she could feel comfortable here. Or so she said."

I giggled. "I must meet her."

"She'll be here for Thanksgiving. She's threatened her old man if he doesn't make it happen, she's coming alone."

I craned my neck to look up at him. "Is that allowed? Threatening your biker badass man into doing your bidding?"

"It won't work for you, but it sometimes works for others."

I snorted. "Oh, I see how it is."

He gave me a gentle squeeze. "Hope you're in the mood for steaks."

"I'm a vegetarian," I said, and bit my lip to keep from giggling.

"Fuck me," he snapped. "You are?"

"Nope." I glanced at him again. "But thanks for being so easy."

Now, this is where I finally figured out that I had to stop shock bombing him because every time I did, I ended up on my back, his hands on my waist, and the very real threat of peeing my pants way too close a reality.

Then, before I actually did soil my drawers, I was kissed to the point of breathlessness, and left wanting more and more. I smiled against his lips and ran my fingers through his hair. "This is really hard."

"Ya think?" he said with a groan. "We can take care of that right now, baby. My bed's incredible."

"It's been a week," I said.

"So?"

"So, it's too soon, Austin. I need to know this is going to last before we jump into bed. I'm not like Kim. I can't have sex and move on."

He dropped his forehead to mine. "We might need to stick to public outings then." He sounded mad.

"Whatever you need," I said.

Austin climbed off me and left me lying on the sofa. I stayed put, listening to him opening cabinets, and then slamming them closed. This lasted for a little while... until I felt like I could talk to him without yelling or crying. I sat up and unzipped my boots, removing them before padding into the kitchen.

"Can we talk?" I asked, leaning against the island.

"Nothin' to talk about, Dani." Austin opened the fridge and pulled out steaks.

"I disagree. I feel like wanting to wait has made you feel like I don't want you."

He smirked. "Not even close."

"So we're okay?"

"Yeah, babe, we're okay."

"Why don't I believe you?"

He sighed, pausing his chore of seasoning the meat, and studied me. "We're okay, baby. That's part of the problem. You're the sexiest woman I've ever met and I'm having to wait to taste every part of you. The more I know you, the harder it gets... literally. I go to sleep hard, I wake up hard, I jack off in the shower and I'm still fuckin' hard. I hear your voice, I'm hard, I see you smile or hear you laugh, and I'm fuckin' *hard*. It's becoming a problem, Dani."

I forced myself not to squeal in glee. "I'm the sexiest woman you've ever met?"

He shook his head. "I'm standing here talking about my very real medical issue, and you pull that from the conversation."

I bit my lip. "Sorry. No one's ever said that about me before."

"Then you've been hangin' around assholes."

I smiled. "You're probably not wrong."

Austin wiped his hands on a towel and pulled me close, slipping his hands to my bottom and spreading his legs a bit to get down to my level. "You need to be patient with me. I'm gonna get pissed, and I'm probably gonna growl or say somethin' stupid, but it's only because waiting for you is killing me."

"What have you done with other girlfriends?"

He dropped his head back and then focused on me again. "Never had to wait, Dani."

"What? Never? They've just jumped into bed with you?"

"Pretty much."

"Wow. I don't really know what to say to that."

"Different worlds, baby." He smiled. "And you finding your way to mine just rocked it."

I chuckled. "You have such a way with words."

He kissed my nose. "Now, I'm gonna rock yours with these steaks."

"Rock away, honey."

He let me go and true to his word, rocked my world before he took me home and kissed me chastely on my porch. That part had pretty much sucked my world, but I had to stick to my guns or I'd be pregnant the second he touched me.

NINE

Danielle

THE SATURDAY MORNING of girls' night out, I was awoken by the shrill, annoying ring of my burner phone. It was just over a week since I'd figured out I was in trouble and, although I hadn't seen Austin as often as I would have liked, it was enough to confirm my doom. I was falling hard and fast for the man.

"Hello?" I answered, sleepily.

"Did I wake you?" Austin asked.

I smiled. "Yeah, you did."

"You sound sexy as hell in the morning."

"Charmer," I retorted. "What time is it?"

"Ten."

"Honey," I said with a groan. "It's too early."

"So, if I'm at your door with breakfast, you'd tell me to piss off?"

I yawned, snuggling further into my mattress. "You're not really at my door with breakfast, are you?"

"I'm really at your door with breakfast."

I sat up, my hair falling around my face. "Seriously?"

"Yeah, babe, I'm here."

"Crap, honey, I'm a mess. I have bed head and haven't brushed my teeth."

He laughed. "I don't care. Come let me in."

"I will unlock the door, but you have to give me time to get back to my room so I can at least clean up."

"Jesus, Dani, I don't care what you look like."

"But I do. Promise me," I pressed.

"I will give you ten seconds."

I groaned.

"Baby, I got hot coffee and fresh bagels. How long you gonna make me wait?"

I threw the covers off and slid from the mattress. "Poppy seed?"

"You like poppy seed?"

"I love poppy seed."

"Well, shit. I have one of those and a plain. I was kinda hoping you'd go for the plain."

I pulled on a pair of sweats... hard to do with one hand, then made my way to the front door. "You can have the poppy seed," I said.

"Gorgeous *and* generous," he said.

"Okay, I'm unlocking. Count to ten and then come in."

"You're assuming I *can* count to ten," he challenged.

"Hey, you're the one with the high IQ." I giggled. "Ready?"

"Ready, baby."

I glanced in the peephole, saw him standing outside, and bit my lip as I turned the locks and made a mad dash back to my bedroom. I closed the door and stepped into the bathroom. The way my apartment was set up was that there was a pocket door from my bedroom into the bathroom and a door from the hallway into the same bathroom. I locked the door that led to the hallway and then went about making myself presentable.

After washing my face, brushing my teeth, and pulling my hair into a simple ponytail, I pulled on fresh undies and a pair of yoga pants that I knew did great things for my butt. I donned a shelf cami and a T-shirt and then made my way to the kitchen.

Austin was rummaging through my fridge, but he'd laid the breakfast goodies on a paper bag and when I saw the logo, I clapped my hands. "Noah's?"

He closed the fridge and faced me, letting out a quiet, "Fuck," before rushing me. His mouth slammed onto mine and his tongue swept inside, making me hungry in a completely different way. I slid my hands up his chest and stroked his neck, letting the feeling of his body pressed against mine sink in. He broke the kiss and I grinned. "Well, good morning to you too."

"God, baby, you're gorgeous," he rasped, kissing my neck. He kissed my lips one more time and then let me go. "I didn't know how you liked your coffee, so I just grabbed black."

"Three sugars and lots of cream," I said.

"Good thing I brought lots of cream, then." He held up little containers of half-and-half.

"What about you?

He smiled. "Just black, babe."

"You're easy."

He chuckled and grabbed the plain bagel. "Depends on who you ask."

I grinned.

"You still have nothing in your fridge," he pointed out.

"I know. You've been a bad influence and distraction. I really need to go shopping." I grabbed the sugar from the cabinet above the dishwasher and spooned some into my cup.

Austin handed me a bagel.

"I thought you wanted the poppy seed," I said as Austin spread cream cheese on the plain one.

He shook his head. "It's all you, babe."

"You're pulling out all the charm today, aren't you?"

He leaned down to kiss me quickly. "Not just today. You'll see."

"Promises, promises." I followed him to the table. "What are you doing here? I thought we weren't seeing each other today."

"I moved a few things around so I could drive you and your friend tonight."

"What?"

"I'm your shuttle service," he said. "Wherever you need to go, I'll take you."

"I don't need you to drive me," I pointed out. "I have a car that runs better than ever, thanks to you."

He took a sip of his coffee. "Yeah, but if I take you, you can drink whatever you want and not worry about driving."

"There is that." I raised an eyebrow. "We might be really late, though. We typically are."

Austin smiled. "What time do you want me to pick you up?"

"I haven't worked that out yet. Kim knows not to call me before eleven. Even if she were dying, she'd have to wait until after then to let me know."

He shot me a sexy little smirk. "I'm not apologizing for wakin' you, babe. It made my day."

I lifted my bagel. "I'll take this as one even so."

"Knock yourself out."

"You really want to drive us tonight?"

He nodded.

"You're sure you're not busy?" I asked.

"Nothin' I can't move, baby."

I tilted my head and stared at him in suspicion. "What's your game, mister?"

Austin laughed. "Just want to take care of my woman. Make sure she's safe."

I leaned forward and kissed him quickly. "Thank you."

"You're welcome."

We sat silently chewing for a few minutes before my phone pealed from the bedroom. I rose to my feet. "That might be Kim." I rushed for my room and grabbed the phone just in time. "This is Dani."

"Someone's awake early," Kim said. "I was expecting to leave a message."

"Austin brought me breakfast."

"Wow, you must really like this guy. No one wakes you on the weekend without feeling your wrath."

I giggled. "I'm not *that* bad."

"You keep telling yourself that, honey."

"So what's the plan for tonight?" I asked, and headed back to the dining area. Austin had moved to my sofa, his booted feet up on my coffee table, the remote in his hand.

"How about I pick you up at nine and we head to Blush?"

"Hoping if we get there a little earlier, we'll be able to get in?"

Kim laughed. "That's the plan."

"I like it. Just one change."

"What?"

"Austin wants to drive. So, how about we pick you up?"

"He's crashing girls' night?" she asked.

"Nope. He's just designated driver. He'll drop us wherever we want to go and pick us up when we're done. It means we can drink and not worry about getting a cab."

"But he's not staying."

I glanced at Austin. "Nope, he's not staying. It's just us."

He raised an eyebrow and cocked his head.

"Sounds good to me," Kim said.

"Awesome. We'll see you at nine."

"Perfect."

I hung up and looked at Austin. "What?"

"What if I want to stay?"

I shook my head and grabbed my bagel, flopping down beside him on the couch. "Resist the urge. It's girls' night out and girls' night out is sacred."

"Where am I taking you?"

"Blush."

"No."

"What?"

"Sorry, let me rephrase," he said. "Hell, no."

I paused mid-chew. "You're joking."

"You're not going to Blush, Dani. It's a meat market."

"It's the most exclusive club in Portland and we've never been able to get in."

"No mystery there, babe. They probably know who you are."

"What's that supposed to mean?"

He scowled.

"Tell me," I demanded.

"Damn it," he said, but didn't elaborate.

I set my bagel on the coffee table and turned to face him. "Austin, what aren't you telling me?"

"Club business."

"So, this is how it's going to go every time you don't want to tell me something? You're going to hide behind 'club business'?"

"Babe, I can't tell you. You just have to pick somewhere else to go."

"No. We want to go to Blush and since girls' night out

is sacred, you don't get a say in it. If you want to drive us, you can take us where we want to go."

"Blush is off the table, Dani."

"Then we'll get a cab."

He studied me. "I'm driving you, babe, *and* you're going somewhere other than Blush."

I threw my hands up in frustration. "You are not the boss of me, Austin!"

His phone buzzed and he swore again, but answered it after he checked the caller ID. "Yo. Yeah. Fuck me. This shit needs to be dealt with, brother." He rose to his feet and headed out my door just like he had the other night. Only, this time, I didn't really want to let him back in. I took my minute of reprieve and called Kim.

"Wow, two calls before eleven," she said. "I must be special."

"Hey. Austin's being all alpha male about Blush and won't 'allow' me to go."

"What the hell?"

"Yep. So, either we go early and blow him off, which I have a feeling won't work, because he's here and I don't really know when he's leaving."

"Or..." Kim said.

"Or, he drops us off somewhere else and we either walk or cab it back to Blush."

Kim chuckled. "You really want to play that game this early in your relationship?"

"*Please*, if he keeps going like this, there isn't going to *be* a relationship."

"Well, I'm up for whatever. I really do want to try for Blush, though."

"Me too," I said. "Okay, it's sorted. I might call you later to fake make plans, you good with that?"

"I got your back, Dani. Always."

"This is why I love you best," I said.

"Okay, I'm going for a run. Love you."

"Love you too." I hung up, finished my bagel, and was downing my last gulp of coffee when Austin walked back in. "Everything okay?"

"Yeah," he said, but I didn't believe him. He looked pissed. "But I have to go."

"Okay. See ya."

"Don't be like that, Dani." He frowned. "Just trust me on the Blush thing."

"You got it, buddy," I quipped, and stood.

He narrowed his eyes and gripped my chin, albeit gently. "Don't go thinkin' you're gonna do anything stupid, Dani."

"Oh, but you said I'm *not* stupid, so how could I possibly *do* anything stupid?"

"Do I need to put a recruit on you?"

"What does that even mean?"

"Have someone watch you."

I gasped and pulled out of his grip. "You *wouldn't*."

"I would if I felt I needed to."

"You know you just erased the experience of a sweet morning breakfast, with me regretting I let you in my house because you're being the biggest dick on the planet."

"When you see mine, babe, you'll see how right you are."

I snorted. "You're disgusting."

"Unfortunately for you, I can't stick around and show you just how fun disgusting can be. I'll pick you up at eight."

"Don't bother," I snapped.

He chuckled, sliding his hand to my neck and pulling my head forward. "Eight o'clock, baby." He kissed me quickly and then he was gone.

I stood next to my couch and stared at the door, debating on whether or not I was going to throw something at it. In the end, I locked up and put a new plan into motion. Austin Carver was going to find out just how dangerous the wrath of Dani could be. Starting with me not being at his beck and call. Jerk!

TEN

Danielle

KIM PICKED ME up at seven and we decided to grab dinner before we headed to the club. My best friend could only be described as perfect. There really was no other way around it. She was tall, almost five-foot-ten, with legs that went on for miles and the ability to wear anything as though it had been made for her. She had long dark hair that never dulled... ever. Big brown eyes and full lips that any woman would die for, and a super sweet way about her. She was as close to me as Emily was, and for all intents and purposes, I considered her my other sister.

Tonight she wore a little black dress that ended just below her butt. How she sat without flashing anyone, I have no idea, but she was a pro at it. Her four-inch Jimmy Choos were silver and strappy and gorgeous, and she wore several varying shades of silver bangles on her left wrist. With her big hair and smoky make-up, she looked more runway model than bartender, and normally, I'd feel ugly beside her. But tonight, I didn't.

I wore a clingy black dress that was low-cut... and I mean, *low*. The hem fell just below my knees and my three-inch black ankle boots did incredible things for my calves. I was all about accentuating the positive and thank God for Spanx, because everything was where it was supposed to be. I had curled my hair in waves, and it hung down perfectly with the help of copious amounts of hairspray, and my big hoop, silver earrings were just enough bling to pull the whole thing together.

As we arrived at the restaurant, I was liking the looks a few men were giving us and I was no longer seething with righteous anger by the time we sat down to eat... just smug with having thwarted my nemesis.

"So, let me get this straight," Kim said. "You've made some drop-dead gorgeous biker fall in love with you, pissed off said biker, and thrown down the wrath of Dani all in less than a couple of weeks."

I raised my pomegranate martini in a toast. "Yay me."

She tapped her glass to mine and laughed. "I cannot *wait* to meet this guy."

"Huh-uh." I shook my head. "You're not going to meet him, Kimmie."

"What? Why not?"

"Because I'm not dating some guy who treats me like chattel. I'm a grown woman, not some little girl who has to do what my big, bad man tells me to." I sipped my drink. "Hell, no. Not gonna happen."

"Amen, sista," Kim retorted.

Our dinner arrived and we giggled through our meal. For the first time in a while, I wasn't feeling like the world was on my shoulders. It was awesome. We grabbed a cab from the restaurant to the club and arrived just as people were beginning to line up.

"Perfect timing," I said.

Kim linked her arm with mine. "Totally."

We walked up the stairs behind two of the most beautiful women I'd ever seen. They were denied entry and my heart dropped. If they couldn't get in, there was no way in hell we were going to.

I handed the bouncer my ID and he glanced at me, then back at the ID. The other guy took Kim's. The men shared a look and then the door was opened for us.

"Welcome," the smaller of the two said.

"Seriously?" I blurted.

"Thanks," Kim said quickly, and pushed me inside.

"I can't believe we're in," I said, and grabbed her hand.

"I picked up on that when you almost made the bouncer change his mind."

I gasped. "I did *not*."

She grinned and we walked further into the club. A half-dressed woman led us to the booth in a corner facing the dance floor. She wore a teeny-tiny black mini skirt with a blood red top that tied at her neck and left her midriff bare. Her bright red stilettos oozed sex appeal, but all I could think about was how she managed to stay on her feet all night. I was already dying in my boots.

I took a minute to take in the space. It was swanky for sure, with red booths, deep mahogany wooden tables and two bars downstairs. Roped off stairs led to the exclusive VIP area that reportedly only the rich of the rich, and/or celebrities were ever granted access.

The dance floor's tiles lit up with multi-colored lights, while the DJ sat on a dais above the dance floor and was currently playing some God-awful dub step piece.

We slid into the booth and the server took our drink

order. I leaned over to Kim and raised an eyebrow. "I thought it would be different in a weird way."

She nodded. "Yeah. I'm hoping we're not going to have to listen to this crap all night. I'll lose my mind."

I giggled. "Me too."

The server returned with our drinks and smiled. "Compliments of the gentlemen sitting over there," she said, and pointed to the booth across the dance floor from us.

"Thank you," I said.

The men were cute. Both clean cut, both dark haired. Both dressed in tailored suits, sans ties. One was sporting the perfect amount of stubble on his face to give him a hint of sexy and mysterious, while the other was clean-shaven.

Neither of them made me think of Austin. Not at all. They didn't make me think of his face that was soft to the touch, or the fact that just that morning, he'd obviously not had the chance to shave, so he left my mouth deliciously chafed. They didn't make me think of the jeans that fit him perfectly or the smell of his leather cut when I'd dropped my cheek to his chest. I was well and truly perfectly capable of putting all my thoughts of Austin 'Booker' Carver out of my mind.

We took the drinks and tipped them toward the men in thanks and then sipped.

"Wow, that's a cocktail," Kim said, and set her drink down.

"Yes, yes, it is." I felt my purse buzz and opened it to locate my phone. "Well, looky here. Six missed calls from Austin... oh, and...," I giggled, "... a couple of very irritated texts."

"Seriously?" Kim sipped her drink again.

"Yep. 'Where are you?', 'What the hell, Dani,' etcetera, etcetera." I snorted in derision. "I hope this teaches him a lesson. I am not a woman to be messed with." My tipsy mind was making me quite self-assured, and I threw the phone back in my purse and focused on my drink again.

The song changed and I gasped. "I love this song! Let's dance."

I dragged Kim onto the dance floor where several other people were congregating. I was apparently not the only one who loved this song. What could I say? Pink was always a good dance choice.

I don't know how long we stayed on the floor. At least three songs, before I was feeling stifled by the body heat and in desperate need of water. We made our way back to the table and our server brought us both water and fresh drinks. Again, compliments of the gentlemen across from us. This time, however, they made their way to our table and slid in beside us.

"Ladies," the one with the stubble crooned to me. His friend sat next to Kim, leaving us in the middle and each of them on the ends. Ergo, we had no escape. We were pinned in.

"Hi," I said, nervously.

"I'm Derek," clean-shaven guy said.

"And I'm Aaron."

"Nice to meet you," I said. "I'm Dani and this is Kim. Thank you for the drinks."

Aaron smiled at me. He had a smooth yet sleazy quality about him that I couldn't quite put my finger on. "Our pleasure," he said. "You girls here for anything special?"

I shook my head. "Girls' night out."

Kim was noticeably silent. Totally unlike her, but when I looked her way, she appeared to be warding off Derek, who might as well have had eight arms with how successful she was being.

I looked back at Aaron. "I'm sorry, but we really just came here for some girl time, so thank you for the drinks, but would you mind leaving us alone?"

"Yeah, that's not gonna happen."

"Excuse me?"

"You came here lookin' to meet, and we're meetin', so we'll buy you a couple more drinks if you need them, but we're not going anywhere." He ran his hand up my thigh.

I shoved him away. "You disgusting pervert. You think because you bought us drinks that, might I remind you, neither of us requested, you're due some form of reward?"

"Bitch, you need to learn better manners."

"I believe the lady asked you to leave."

I gasped at the sound of the familiar voice, but when I caught a glimpse of Austin, he wasn't in his signature jeans and cut, he was in a suit that looked expensive. Like Armani kind of expensive.

"Who the hell are you?" Derek demanded.

"We're the ladies' dates," came another voice. Mack revealed himself by walking around Kim's side of the booth, also dressed in a dark suit, complementing his blond hair and adding a whole new level to his sex-appeal.

"Yeah?" Aaron sneered. "Well, we got here first."

That was the last thing either of them said, as Austin grabbed Aaron, and Mack grabbed Derek. They yanked them from the booth and shoved them to the back. The whole incident took less than a minute. Kim and I were left with our mouths agape, and my heart raced with a nervous intensity.

"Who the hell were they?" she asked.

"Austin and Mack," I replied.

"I thought you said they were bikers."

I groaned. "They are!"

"Holy shit, Dani. You didn't say they were hot."

"Um, I believe I did."

"But you didn't say they were *hawt*!"

"Hey, Kim," I droned. "Austin and his friend are hawt."

"No kidding."

114

Before I could comment further, my arm was squeezed, and Austin was standing beside me again. "Come with me."

"No."

"Dani," he warned.

"What are you doing here?" I demanded.

"Come." He tugged on my arm, pulling me toward him. "With. Me."

"No," I pulled out of his hold. "I'm here with Kim and we're having a good time."

"Being pawed by a couple of grade A douchebags is a good time?" he challenged.

"We could have handled it," I said with a little more confidence than I felt at the time.

He leaned forward so his mouth was against my ear. "Get the fuck out of the booth and come with me Dani, or I swear to God, I will remove you."

I gasped and glanced at Kim who was being schmoozed by Mack... the traitor. He did look frickin' delicious, but still, she should have been as mad as I was.

Austin held out his hand and I slid from the booth, ignoring him, and stepping toward Kim. "Hi, Mack. You look really nice."

"Thanks, babe," he said, sending a smirk over my shoulder, and then focusing back on me again. "So do you."

Austin's hand settled on my lower back and I was being guided (pushed) to where he wanted me to go, which was toward the back of the club. He walked me down a dimly-lit hallway and through the fourth door on the right (I know this for sure, because I counted).

The room was surprisingly warm with the same mahogany finishings as the club, but instead of the red leather booths, there was an overstuffed sofa, flat screen television and a desk in the corner. I heard the door click behind me and I turned to face Austin. "Where's Kim?"

"Mack's taking her home."

"What? Why? You have no right to blow up girls' night, Austin."

He crossed his arms and frowned. "I told you not to come here tonight, Dani. Told you I'd pick you up and take you anywhere else you wanted to go. What the fuck?"

"It's a nice place. I don't know what your problem is. We got in, which is somewhat of a miracle to begin with, so I was looking forward to having a good time."

"You got in because I let you in."

"What?" I squeaked.

"The Dogs own it, babe. I run it."

"What?" I repeated.

He sighed. "I told Tommy and Tiny to watch for you and Kim."

"What?" I threw my purse on the sofa. "So are you saying you've known who I was all along?"

"No, babe. I have two rules. No troublemakers or good girls. Nothing will get a club in hot water faster."

"How could you possibly—"

"Have you ever gotten in?"

"Well, no," I conceded.

"You would have been denied access because my team is good. Better than good. And they would have seen you coming from a mile away. No one looked close enough at you for your name to raise any red flags. Harris isn't an uncommon last name and your father and brother work out of Washington."

He had a point.

"So, they don't know I'm a cop's daughter?"

"They do now."

"Is that why you're here? To make sure I don't tell my daddy?" I snapped.

"You're here, because tonight's the worst fucking night for you to be here."

"Why?"

"Club—"

"Business. I get it." I scowled. "God, Austin, I'm so frickin' sick of hearing that."

He pulled his phone out of his pocket. "Yo."

I hadn't even heard it buzz. I stomped my foot in frustration. I guess our conversation was over.

"Yeah. Two minutes." He hung up. "Wait here. Got me?"

"No. I'm not a child, Austin. You don't get to leave me here like I'm being relegated to the principal's office."

He swore and stormed out of the office. I moved to follow but the door was locked. I let out a frustrated squeal and kicked the door, only managing to stub my toe.

"I swear to God, Austin Carver, I'm going to castrate you," I yelled at the door, and then flopped onto the sofa and pulled my phone from my purse to call Kim.

"Hey, honey," Kim said.

"Hey, where are you?" I asked.

"Just crossed the bridge."

"I'm so sorry Austin's such a killjoy."

Kim chuckled. "Don't worry about it."

"Are you okay?"

"I'm totally fine, hon. Seriously, it's all good. I'll call you tomorrow okay?"

I frowned. Was she blowing me off too? "Um, okay."

"'Bye."

She hung up and I sat staring at my phone for several seconds before chucking it back into my purse. My girdled middle was uncomfortable, so I wrestled my Spanx from my body, then I unzipped my boots and slid them off. My toe was throbbing now, but I stood and decided to investigate the space.

A pocket door led to a spacious bathroom, complete with shower and fluffy towels. I wondered how often Austin stayed here long enough to shower. I walked back into the office and through another door to find a bar set up with several chairs surrounding small tables. What had me spellbound was a large picture window that overlooked the entire club. I didn't remember seeing it when I was out there, so wondered if it was a one-way mirror.

I'm not sure how long I stood watching the club goers, hearing nothing but my own breathing, but Austin's arm wrapping around my waist startled me and I jumped.

He kissed my temple. "Sorry, baby. I didn't mean to scare you."

I pulled away from him. "I want to go home now. Will you call me a cab?"

"No."

"Why not?"

"I'll take you home, but I can't leave just yet. We've got a situation and I don't know how long it's gonna take."

"Which part of I want to be alone are you not picking up on?"

He slid his hand to my neck and tipped my chin up with his thumb. "You and I have things to talk about. I get that. But you're not leaving without me, Dani, so accept that now."

"God, you make me so frickin' crazy!"

"And you're a pain in the ass."

"So, let me leave!"

He stared at me and then his mouth covered mine slowly. I was so wound up, I reacted with pure unadulterated lust, opening my mouth and deepening the kiss, while moving my hands to his hair. When his hand pulled my dress up and slid between my legs, I whimpered with need. He slid my panties aside and slipped his fingers inside of me while working my clit with his thumb. "Fuck," he rasped. "You're so wet."

I dropped my hands and shimmied my panties down my hips, kicking them to the side. "Take care of that, will you?"

He dropped to his knees in front of me, sliding my

dress to my waist, and pressing his mouth to my clit. "Spread, baby."

I spread my legs a little more and he wrapped one arm around me to hold me still. He thrust two fingers inside of me, sucking my clit until he'd apparently decided I'd had enough. He stood, lifting me in his arms, carrying me to the office and laying me on the sofa. He tapped one of my knees and I dropped it so he could return to what he was doing before. God, what this man could do with his tongue. I tilted my hips in an effort to get closer.

"Fuckin' soaked," he said, and slipped his fingers inside me again.

I felt my climax build as his mouth covered my center and I gripped his hair as my orgasm hit. Austin kissed my inner thighs, slid his fingers out of me and rose to his feet. I watched through hooded eyes as he walked into the bathroom and washed up.

ELEVEN

Danielle

I COULD BARELY move, but I managed to slide my dress back down to cover my nakedness and roll onto my side. Austin walked back toward me and I saw the rock-hard evidence of his arousal pressing against his zipper, but I was disappointed to discover that we weren't going any further. At least not right at the moment.

"I have to get back downstairs." He sat down next to me and smiled as he stroked my cheek. "More of this later."

"I want to yell at you right now, but I can't move." I slid my hand up his leg. "Give me a few minutes and I'll be back to fighting form."

Austin grinned, leaning down to kiss me quickly. "If

you need anything, press the button by the door. Someone will assist you. But no one's gonna let you leave, Dani, so don't bother trying."

"See? Now you're pissing me off again." I scowled. "You're essentially keeping me prisoner and not telling me why."

"I can't tell you why."

"I know, club business," I ground out.

He sighed and rose to his feet. "I have to go."

"Fine, go." I closed my eyes and forced back my frustration as he walked out the door.

I didn't get up until my bladder insisted I move, so I did. After that, I wandered back into the bar area, found my panties, and slid them back on. Surveying the racks of alcohol, I found what looked like really good Tequila and opened the bottle. Common sense would have suggested I pour a shot or two, or even mix the spirit with coke, however, I wasn't feeling very common sensy, so I decided to drink directly from the bottle. And it was fantastic.

I'd taken a couple of long pulls from the bottle and figured I should find some food, so I pressed the little button by the door. Then I pressed it again and again, giggling maniacally as I did it again… then once more, just for fun.

"You only need to ring once, Miss Harris," a female voice came through the little speaker above the button. "What can I get for you?"

"Well, since I'm drinking, I think I should eat something."

"Good idea. What would you like?"

"Filet mignon, medium rare with braised asparagus and garlic mashed potatoes," I rattled off.

"As you wish."

"Wait, I was kidding," I jumped to say. "Can you really do that?"

"We can do whatever you'd like, Miss Harris."

121

"Well, okay. Um, how about some hummus and pita, please?" I asked.

"Of course."

"Thank you," I said, and sat back on the sofa, taking another swig of my delicious drink.

Ten minutes later, the door opened, and a young, good-looking man walked in with my food. I saw the open door and glanced at him.

He smiled. "Please don't try, Miss Harris. You won't get far, and you'll just make Mr. Carver angry."

I scowled. "I think I could take you."

"You could try." He chuckled. "I see you found the Barrique de Ponciano Porfidio."

"Huh?"

He pointed to the bottle of tequila.

"Oh, yes," I said. "The tequila."

"The two-thousand-dollar bottle of tequila."

"Shut up!" I added in a whisper, "Is it really?"

He chuckled with a nod. "Enjoy your refreshments, Miss Harris."

And then he was gone. I flopped back onto the sofa and grabbed a piece of flatbread, scooping the warm hummus onto it and devouring it within seconds. I couldn't remember a time I'd ever tasted anything better and I knew it wasn't just because I was rapidly approaching drunkenness. It was damn good food.

I took another few bites before sitting back and evaluating my current state. I decided it would be a good idea to take a break from the tequila and maybe rest a bit. My head was foggy and I was no longer feeling tipsy and happy. I was rapidly approaching drunk… that is, if I wasn't already… and I was back to feeling frustrated and angry.

I couldn't believe that Austin would just leave me here. He had no right. I walked to the button again and this time a man's voice came over the loudspeaker.

"Will someone let me know when I'll be released from

my cell?" I asked.

"Mister Carver didn't give me that information, Miss Harris. I'm sorry."

"Well, tell Aus—*Mister* Carver that if someone doesn't fill me in on what the hell is going on, I'm going to call my brother."

No one responded, so I decided to give them five minutes before I was going to pull out my cell phone and call down the wrath of Dani in the form of Elliot Harris, badass detective with a heart of gold. I giggled at the thought. Maybe I should switch careers. Be an ad person. My brilliance was obviously wasted on five-year-olds.

I was pulled from my thoughts when Austin walked into the room. "What the fuck, Dani?"

"You got my message I see," I slurred, swaying a little on my feet.

"I can't deal with you right now."

"Then let me go *home!*" I snapped.

He swept past me and grabbed my purse. Taking my cell out of it, he slid the device into his pocket.

"What are you doing?" I squeaked.

"Protecting you from yourself."

I forced back tears of frustration. "I hate you so much right now."

He sighed. Making his way to the door, he opened it, handed my phone to who the hell knows, nodded, and then closed the door again. He pulled me into his arms and stroked my hair. "I know you don't get what's happening, baby, and if I could explain it, I would. But I need you to trust me." He lifted my chin. "I'm trying to keep you safe."

"By having me locked up in a strange place?"

"By having you close." He cupped my cheek. "Please, Dani. Trust that I've got your back. Kim's safe—"

"Was she not safe before?" I demanded.

"That's something I wasn't willing to find out. Mack's

got her."

I snorted. "Knowing Kim, Mack's probably tied up to the bed while she fucks him senseless."

Austin burst out laughing. "Babe."

"What? It's true. She's perfect and awesome and sweet, but she loves sex and she goes through men like underwear." I shrugged. "They love every minute of it, but she doesn't tend to stay with one guy for very long."

"Well, knowing Mack, he'll be happy to oblige whatever fantasy she can dream up."

I licked my lips. "Can I really not go home?"

"Not right now. I *will* make this up to you, but if you'll just be patient for a little while longer, I'd appreciate it."

"I drank your two-thousand-dollar tequila," I challenged.

"I know."

"You're not mad?"

He smiled. "No, baby, I'm not mad. Just pace yourself."

"It made me tired."

"I bet."

"It also made me horny." I bit my lip, sliding my hand under the waistband of his trousers.

"Fuck, baby," he rasped, grabbing my wrist. "I can't do this right now."

"Five minutes," I argued.

"No." He cupped my face. "One, I'm not having our first night together be when you're wasted out of your mind and, two, I have shit to do." He turned away from me and opened a cabinet door against the wall. Pulling out a blanket and pillow, he dropped them on the sofa and then closed the distance between us again. "Hydrate, Dani, okay? If you get tired, go to sleep. I don't know how long this is going to take. If you want to watch television, do so. Do your best to make yourself at home and if you need anything, press the button. But try not to pull me away again, yeah? I need to focus."

"Fine. Go." I pulled away and flopped onto the couch.

He sighed again and leaned down. "Rest, baby. You'll feel better once you sleep off the alcohol."

"Do I need to remind you of the fact you're not the boss of me?" I asked.

Austin smiled. "God, you're gorgeous."

"Don't get all cute and sexy right now, Austin Carver. I'm not in the mood."

He kissed my forehead. "Forgive me. I'll see you in a bit."

I waved my hand in the air and stuck my tongue out at him. "'Bye. Don't let the door hit ya where the good Lord split ya."

He grinned and walked out the door.

TWELVE

Booker

I LOCKED THE door behind me and nodded to one of my youngest recruits, Train, who was on Danielle watch. Train was nineteen, six-foot-five, and quite possibly the size of a small house. Hence his name. If he hit you, it would be akin to being hit by a freight train. I trusted him with Danielle because Train wouldn't let anyone past him, and he was wholly loyal to me.

I headed back downstairs, and Johnny met me at the door to the basement. The club's basement was sometimes referred to as the "Woodshed," as it was here that lessons that could only be learned with a switch were dispensed.

Johnny was Blush muscle, but he had no ties to the Dogs, which meant he only knew what I wanted him to know, and it was all under the guise of Blush business.

"Everything okay, boss?" Johnny asked.

I nodded. "You find him?"

"Yeah. He's in the galley."

I headed to the last room on the left, stepping inside the long narrow space, and closing the door behind me. Steven Mills. The man who ruined Dani's life was duct-taped to a chair in the middle of the room, my laptop open on the table beside him, and one of the Dogs' soldiers, Grizz, keeping guard.

"I apologize for keeping you waiting," I said, and yanked the tape from his mouth.

"Who are you? What do you want?" Steven demanded.

He didn't seem afraid which interested me. I smiled slowly and leaned against the table. "I want to know where the money is."

"And what money would that be?"

I chuckled. "The money you've been stealing from un-suspecting women for the last twelve years."

Steven grinned. "There's only been one."

"No," I corrected. "There's only been one where you've been caught. I have uncovered eight others."

"How the hell did you do that?" Steven snapped.

"That's not really important." I reached back and grabbed a stack of paper. "But I think the D.A. would be interested in learning about them, wouldn't they?"

"Fuck you."

"Sorry, wrong team," I retorted as I thumbed through my research. "You've managed to hide four-point-seven million dollars and I'd like to know where it is."

"Since I don't know what the hell you're talking about, I can't help you."

"I will find the money, Mr. Mills." I slapped the file on the table. "You can count on it. What you can also count on is that this will go easier for you if you just tell me where it is."

Steven shook his head. "What if I could give you something more valuable?"

"Like?"

"Like a notorious motorcycle club President's daughter or perhaps a certain chief of police's daughter, among others?"

I forced myself not to react. Blush couldn't be traced back to the Dogs, I'd made sure of it, but it was still owned by a shell company that owned other businesses in the area. Different than Big Ernie's which *could* be traced back to the Dogs. "Motorcycle club?"

Steven smiled smugly. "Yeah. Some guy with a bird's name... Crow, I think. I'd need to check my records."

I picked up and studied the file in front of me again to keep myself from beating the shit out of Steven. "And why would this be important to me?"

"I get the impression you want money. I can give it to you."

"And the cop's daughter?"

Steven chuckled. "She's this little uptight bitch whose great-grandfather practically built Vancouver and they're loaded."

I took a deep breath. "I'm still not seeing how these women are more valuable than four-point-seven million."

"They have K&R insurance on their kids. The bird guy's kid's worth four mil, but the chief of police has three kids, and each are over ten mil each. You won't get close to two of them, but Dani lives alone and doesn't own a gun. She's a lousy lay, but shit, she's gullible as hell."

I fisted my hand at my side. "And how do you know this?"

"I found it while borrowing Danielle's information. I don't even think she knows about it, but I found it, so you can bet someone else will be able to as well. Find some asshole to snatch these people, keep them somewhere isolated and collect the money. Easy."

I studied him. I'd done a thorough vet of Steven Mills. I'd even found the money he'd stolen, although, it was going to take more to get access to it if Steven didn't offer up the codes. But I wasn't finished with Danielle's background check...I always did checks on the women I slept with...or planned to sleep with...so the kidnap and ransom insurance hadn't pinged yet.

Steven was right. If an asshole like him could find this information, someone else could as well.

This put Dani in an even more vulnerable position than I had originally thought. Shit. I was going to have to get her brother involved.

"Grizz, take care of Mr. Mills for me."

"What the hell does that mean?" Steven bellowed.

I headed back toward the door, but glanced back. "Don't kill him, Grizz. Got me?"

"Yeah. I got you," Grizz said. "Fuckin' pissed about it though."

I chuckled. "Maybe next time."

I walked out of the room to the sound of Steven's squeals of fear. I knew Grizz would rough him up enough to scare him, but not go much further than that. I pulled my phone out of my pocket and dialed Mack.

"Yo."

"Can you talk?" I asked.

"Yeah, give me a sec."

I heard several voices in the background and I figured Mack had headed over to the honky tonk. I wondered how Kim felt about that, considering Mack was gonna take her with him.

"I'm good," Mack said.

"Need you to find out if Kim has a key to Dani's place and then get over there and pack her a bag. Enough for a couple of weeks," I ordered. "Bring it to the club. If not, I'll have Train meet you at her place with a key."

"No problem. It's bad?"

"Worse than I thought. Fuckin' parents have K&R insurance on their kids. Ten mil each."

"Fuck me, seriously?" Mack said.

"Seriously." I rubbed my forehead. "What I need to find out is if anyone else knows that. Keep an eye on the sister, yeah? Her name's Emily. The brother can take care of himself."

"I'll take care of things on my end and text you."

"Thanks, brother."

"'Bye."

I hung up. I was missing something. I just wasn't sure what. My entire plan to get Dani's money and reputation back had taken me down a rabbit hole that was leading me to a place I wasn't prepared to go. A place that could collide with club business.

THIRTEEN

Danielle

I VAGUELY REMEMBER being lifted and carried, the familiar scent of Austin filling my senses as I buried my face in his neck, but then I woke up in a strange bed and had no idea how I'd gotten there.

The light from the moon shone through the window and it gave me enough of a visual to see that there was bottled water on the nightstand, which I opened and drank greedily. My head was pounding, but not quite as badly as I probably deserved. The small blessings of very expensive tequila.

I threw the covers off and realized I was virtually naked. I had on a T-shirt unfamiliar to me, but it smelled like Austin, so I deduced it was his. My panties were in place, but nothing else.

"Babe," Austin grumbled.

I started a little and looked behind me. I hadn't even noticed him in bed beside me.

"Bathroom," I whispered.

He pointed to the door to the right of the bed.

I headed to the bathroom and flipped on the light. Talk about a room you'd never have to leave. A large tile shower big enough for forty-two thousand people (really... not kidding) and six (counted 'em... six) shower heads. Two sinks were nestled in a long vanity with gorgeous cherry wood cabinetry. The heated tile floor felt amazing under my feet and I passed a huge soaking tub on my way to the little room that housed the toilet. After doing my business I took a minute to study my reflection. God, I looked awful.

"Dani?" Austin called. I was grateful he didn't come in. "Babe?"

"Just a minute."

"You okay?"

"Other than looking like a zombie, I'm great."

He chuckled. "I doubt it's all that bad."

"I wish I had my makeup remover."

"Check the medicine cabinet," he called.

I pulled it open and found all of my favorite face creams, toners, cotton rounds, and toothbrush and toothpaste.

"Towels under the sink," Austin said.

"Thanks."

I took a few minutes to freshen up and then padded back into the bedroom. I was alone, so I grabbed a towel, wrapped it around my waist, and went looking for him. I found him in the kitchen, a bottle of ibuprofen in his hand. "How do you feel?" he asked, all sexy like wearing only a pair of cotton pajama bottoms.

"Hung over," I said. "What time is it?"

"Four."

"In the *morning*?"

"Yeah, babe."

"I never wake up this early," I complained.

"Probably the alcohol." He chuckled. "Like your outfit."

"I seem to be missing my clothes." I glanced down my body. "I'm assuming I can thank you for that."

"You were pretty wasted… figured you'd be more comfortable that way."

I frowned. "Are we going to talk about last night?"

"If you need to."

"Um, yeah, I need to, Austin. You held me against my will and left me to get drunk in a dark, isolated office."

"I did."

"You're not even going to deny it?" I don't know why I was surprised, but I was.

"Nope," he said, and opened the bottle of pain relief.

"I hate you so much right now." I stomped my foot and turned on my heel. "I'm leaving."

I stormed back the way I came, let myself into the bedroom, and made a valiant effort to find my clothes.

"They're not in here, babe."

I turned and scowled at Austin leaning against the doorjamb. "Where are they?"

"Laundry." He pushed away from the door and smiled. "Take these."

I narrowed my eyes at him. "What's your game, mister?"

"No game, baby. Just ibuprofen for your head."

"No, not *that*," I said, taking the pills from him and swallowing them without water. Gross. "Why are my clothes in the laundry? I'm going to have to wear them home, right?"

He shook his head and opened his walk-in closet.

I noticed my suitcase leaning up against the inside wall

and made my way to it. "Why is this here?"

"You're staying with me for a few days."

"What? Why?"

Austin sat on the edge of the mattress. "There's been a development that I'm uncomfortable with, and since I know you'll be safe here, you're here."

"What kind of development?" I faced him again. "And if you say 'club business,' Austin, I swear to God, I will kill you."

He gave me a slight smile. "I found Steven."

"I'm sorry?"

"And your money."

"What?" I squeaked.

"I also discovered there's a ten-million-dollar kidnap and ransom insurance policy on you."

"*What?*"

"Steven offered you up as an alternative to returning the money he stole from you."

"What?" I said again, only this time it was barely a whisper.

"Come here, baby."

I went to him immediately.

He wrapped his arms around my waist and pulled me between his legs. "I need to talk to your father and brother. I have no idea if there's even a threat yet, but I'm not happy that Steven knew about the insurance and offered it up to me at all, let alone so quickly. For the time being, I want you here where I can protect you."

"Steven was at the club?"

Austin nodded.

I looped my arms around his neck. "That's why you locked me up."

"Partly," he said. "There are other things going on that I can't tell you about, but if it involves you, baby, I won't keep that from you. I was being pulled in a few different directions last night and I knew if you were in my office, you were safe."

"Austin." I sighed and dropped my forehead to his. "I can't say I liked the way you did it, but I will give you a little grace since you were trying to protect me." He smiled, and I shook my head. "*But*... and this is a big but, so hear me here, honey. If you ever do anything like that again without talking to me first, I will cut you."

He chuckled. "I hear you, baby."

"Come to dinner tomorrow... ah, tonight. You can talk to my brother and dad then."

"They won't mind?"

I shook my head. "I'll call my mom and let her know, but no, they won't mind."

"Gotta meet with Crow and Hatch tomorrow, but it shouldn't conflict."

I nodded and smiled.

He slid his hands under my T-shirt and up my back, kissing my collarbone. "Do you have any idea how gorgeous you are?"

"Not nearly as gorgeous as you," I said, my fingers finding their way into his hair.

He tugged my shirt off and pulled me close again, drawing a nipple into his mouth. I dropped my head back, the feeling heady as he bit down gently. He slid my panties down my hips and I stepped out of them, feeling my way as my nipple was still in his mouth.

His finger slid through the wetness between my legs and then slipped inside of me. I gasped and my hips bucked as he slid another inside me. He wrapped an arm around my waist and guided me onto the bed, his fingers still doing unbelievably incredible things to my body.

"You on the pill?"

I shook my head, gasping as his thumb found my clit. I could feel an orgasm building, but before it washed over me, he removed his hand.

"Austin," I hissed.

He chuckled and I heard a little whoosh of something being torn. "Condom, baby."

He rose up above me, settling his hips between mine and guiding himself inside of me. I wrapped my legs around him and arched up.

"You're tight, baby. Am I hurting you?"

"God, no," I breathed. "More."

He grinned, covering my mouth with his and thrusting deep inside of me.

"Yes," I whispered. "More, honey."

He drew my nipple back into his mouth again as he surged deeper and deeper, faster and faster. I had no warning of my climax as the orgasm washed over me and I cried out his name. Never in my life had I come so fast, so hard, and I gripped his biceps as I caught my breath.

Austin let out a grunt and I felt his cock pulsate inside of me before he rolled us onto our sides, staying connected to me as he wrapped his arms around my waist. "Fuck me," he whispered, and kissed me deeply.

"I think I just did." I grinned and stroked his cheek. "Amazing."

He chuckled. "You have very low expectations, then, baby. This was nothing."

"I think that was my very first orgasm," I whispered.

"What?" He frowned. "Ever?"

I nodded. "I thought I'd had orgasms in the past, but it was never like that. I had no idea what good sex was, I think. I mean, I did, because my sister gave me a broad stroke idea of what good sex could be, but I've never personally experienced it. Not like that."

"Babe," he said, and smiled. "That's a fuckin' crime. You're beautiful all the time, but when you come, God, it's incredible."

I bit my lip. "Can we do it again?"

Austin laughed. "Hell, yeah, we can do it again. I'll take care of the condom. Don't move."

I grimaced when he slid out of me and headed to the bathroom. My body was wired, ready for him to do whatever he wanted to me. So much for my plan to make him wait a while. But ten days was a while, right?

The dip of the bed pulled me from my thoughts, and I smiled up at the man who'd totally ruined me for anyone else.

"I can hear you thinking," he said.

"Just thinking how you've totally ruined me for any other man."

He leaned down and kissed me gently. "There'll never be another man."

"You're so sure, huh?"

Austin nodded. "I love you, Dani."

I gasped and sat up, my forehead almost colliding with his. "What?"

He grinned. "You heard me."

"But you can't."

"Why can't I?"

"It's too soon."

"Is it?"

I let out a frustrated squeak. "Quit volleying with me."

Austin laughed, pulling me down on top of him. "I've had the kind of life that when I find something good, I see it for what it is. I love you. End of story."

I dropped my cheek to his chest. "I don't know what to say."

"Don't have to say anything, babe."

"You're not mad?" I was surprised he was so calm.

"About what?"

"Me not saying it back," I said, lifting my head.

He chuckled. "Why the hell would I be mad?"

I sighed. "I have just always wondered what it would be like to be so secure in one's self that they can say whatever they want and not feel vulnerable and stupid."

"You think I'm vulnerable and stupid?" he teased.

"*No*," I said quickly, and groaned.

Austin rolled me onto my back and slid his hand to my neck, thumbing my pulse. It was his go-to when I was feeling off-kilter, and it always made me feel safe. "Talk to me," he prodded. "You can tell me anything, Dani."

"It was when you warmed my hands," I admitted.

"What was?"

"When I fell in love with you." I squeezed my eyes shut expecting him to tell me I was an idiot.

"Eyes, baby."

I opened them and shivered. He was looking at me as though I'd just given him the most precious gift. "It was when you talked in your sleep," he said.

"Huh?"

"The other night. When you talked in your sleep."

"Oh, right." I groaned. "What did I say?"

He smiled, running a finger between my breasts. "'I love you, Austin. Don't leave me.'"

I gasped. "I did not."

"Swear to God you did."

"Is that why you're telling me all of this?" I asked, scared of what his answer might be.

"Hell, no." He frowned. "Do you really think I'd do that?"

"No idea," I admitted. "I try not to trust my gut because I'm usually wrong."

"Well, just so we're clear, I wouldn't. I will always tell you the truth and if I can't tell you something, I'll say so."

"Deal." I smiled. "Are we done talking now?"

"Would you rather do something else?" he asked.

I bit my lip and nodded.

He grinned, sliding his hand between my legs. "Like?"

I arched my hips and sighed. He pulled his hand away. "Huh-uh. You have to say it, Dani."

My face flamed. "Touch me."

He touched my thigh. "Here?"

"No," I rasped.

He moved his hand to my hip. "Here?"

I shook my head.

"Where, baby?"

"There."

He chuckled. "Not good enough. Tell me what you want me to do to you."

"I want... um... your mouth."

"You want my mouth?"

I nodded and squeezed my eyes shut.

"Eyes, Dani."

I looked at him again and my heart raced.

"Where do you want my mouth?" he asked.

"Down... there."

He smiled, moving his hand to my stomach. "You want my mouth here?"

"Lower," I whispered.

"All you have to do is say it, baby, and I'll give you whatever you want."

"I want your mouth on my... pu... um... pussy."

Austin didn't make me wait as he knelt between my legs and pushed my knees open. Guiding one of my legs over his shoulder, he covered my core with his mouth and sucked my clit, and then blew gently.

I mewed and arched into his mouth as he continued his delicious assault. I vaguely registered the sound of tearing foil and then his girth filled me and I cried out in delight. His thumb had replaced his mouth on my clit, and then he rolled onto his back, carrying me with him so I was straddling him. I anchored my hands on his chest and lowered myself so I could draw him deeper inside of me.

"Babe," he whispered, grabbing my bottom with one hand, while he continued to stroke me with the other.

I raised up and then lowered myself again, the sensation of him filling me while I had all the power incredibly exciting. I raised up again and smiled down at him. "Like this? Am I doing it right, Mr. Carver?" I used my very best, dumb blonde voice, and for whatever reason, his eyes widened and his breathing came in short bursts.

I lowered again and quickly found myself on my back and Austin driving into me so fast and hard, I came before he was done. I cried out and gripped his arms, wrapping my legs around him as he surged forward again and again, building something inside of me I wasn't expecting. I burst into tears as another orgasm hit and he fell on top of me, breathing hard, and his hand going for my neck. "Baby, I'm sorry, did I hurt you?"

I shook my head, unable to stop my sobbing.

"Hey." Austin leaned up and stroked my cheek. "Dani, you're scaring me. Talk to me."

"I can't." My sobs wracked my body and I knew... just *knew*... it was the ugly cry. Like when snot flies out of your nose at the same time as gushing saltwater seeps from your eyeballs and mixes with all manner of bodily fluids to give your face a sheen that no one really wants to see.

I covered my face with my hands and Austin pulled me into the safety of his body and held me, stroking my back until I was able to calm down. The tears dried up, but the hiccupping was on full tilt.

He cupped the back of my head and gently guided my face forward, kissing my forehead. "You okay?"

I nodded, taking a deep breath and then another. "I'm sorry."

"Why are you sorry?"

"Because I'm all snotty and gross."

Austin chuckled. "You're fuckin' adorable, Dani, do you know that?"

"Phlegm turns you on, huh?"

"Only yours, baby."

I shoved my face into his neck. "I was not expecting that."

"Are you sure I didn't hurt you?"

"Positive." I met his eyes. "I just couldn't stop coming and I was so overwhelmed by you. I felt beautiful and loved, and wholly cherished, and it was so much to take in."

"You are all of those things," he said. "I thought I might have scared you. I had a flashback and it made me a little crazy."

"What kind of flashback?"

"The kind that when I dropped you off at your place that first night, I envisioned you in thigh-high stockings, a pearl necklace and those glasses of yours, riding me while I sucked your tits."

I gasped. "You did?"

"Yeah. Spent a few nights alone with my hand while calling up that fantasy."

I shook my head. "You're insane."

"Yep. You make me crazy."

"Ditto." I giggled and leaned forward to kiss his heavily tattooed chest. I was looking forward to exploring every inch of them. "I love your tattoos."

"You do?"

I nodded. "I've never been a big tattoo person, although, they all work on you."

Austin smiled and kissed my forehead. "How's your head?"

"Pounding," I said. "And I'm sleepy."

"Sleep baby. I'll take care of the condom and be right back."

"'K," I said on a yawn.

Austin left me, returning quickly and pulling me into his arms. He kissed my shoulder and I fell asleep almost immediately with a smile on my face.

FOURTEEN

Booker

I WALKED INTO the club, my thoughts occupied by the last few hours. I'd left Dani asleep in my bed, waking her briefly to tell her where I was going, before kissing her and watching as she fell back into slumber.

I'd stopped at the front desk of my building to inform the doorman that Dani was in my apartment and to not let her leave without talking with me first.

I took a minute to grab my mail, running into my neighbor, Macey Stone, a nurse at the local hospital.

"Hey, Booker," Macey said as she thumbed through her mail.

The gorgeous red-head looked like she'd just come in

from a run.

"Hey, Mace. Where's your husband?"

"Dallas got called into work." She wrinkled her nose. "I really wish criminals would be more sensitive to our schedule. I've only had one full day with him this week."

I chuckled. Macey's husband was an FBI agent and that was all I cared to know about him.

"Did I hear you tell Trevor you've got a lady visitor?"

I grinned. "My woman's staying with me for a few days. Her name's Dani."

"Awesome. If I get a chance, I'll go introduce myself." Macey scanned her mail. "Payton's coming over to get the rest of her stuff, so we'll both go."

Payton had been Macey's roommate up until Macey got married.

I smiled. "I think she'd really like that."

"Gotta hit the shower," Macey said. "See ya."

"Bye, babe," I said, and headed to the garage.

"Booker," Crow said, pulling me back to the present.

"Hey." I glanced up to see the Prez with a glass of whiskey in his hand. "Shit, already?"

"Fuckin' shit day, Book."

"Gonna get worse."

"Figured." He started toward the back of the building. "Let's talk in my office."

I kicked the door closed behind me and flopped down in one of the chairs facing Crow's desk. "You got K&R insurance on your kid?"

Crow sat in my office chair and scowled. "How do you know about that?"

"I found out from the asshole who stole Dani's money."

Crow pulled out his cell phone and put it to his ear. "Hatch, I want Flea on Ashley twenty-four-seven. Yeah. I don't give a flyin' fuck if she don't want it, she don't got a choice. Update me. Yeah." He hung up. "Talk to me."

"This douchebag has records on several folks who have insurance policies over two mil, including Dani. He seems mostly interested in kidnap and ransom, but he's got half a dozen accidental death ones as well. I'm diggin' deeper and I've got Train and Grizz on 'im until I can figure out what his game is. I cross-referenced the names on the policies and no one's been kidnapped or killed so far, but I'm thinkin' he wants to benefit from this information, so I'm assuming he'll either act on it or sell it."

"Fuck," Crow said. "You got your woman?"

I nodded. "She's safe. I'm gonna talk to her brother and father and see what they think."

"Tread lightly there."

"No, I'm gonna fill them in on all the club's business, including our not so above-board dealings. Then I'm gonna hand them all the money and hold my hands out for the cuffs."

Crow laughed. "Fuck you, Book."

"Got me a woman I like better, Crow." I grinned. "But thanks for the offer."

Crow sipped his drink. "Anything else?"

I shook my head. "Nope. Don't know if you want to bring this up at church, but figured you could use the next few days to make that call."

"Thanks," he said. "Things good with Hawk?"

"I'm not gonna kill him, if that's what you're askin'."

"Need you two to work this out, Booker. Can't have two of my top men at each other's throats."

"How 'bout you stay the fuck out of it?"

Crow leaned forward, arms on the desk. "Right now, it's not fuckin' with the club, but if it starts to, I'll be gettin' in the fuckin' middle and neither of you'll like it. Get me? And I swear to Christ, if I have to get Hatch involved, it'll be worse."

I nodded, stamping down my irritation.

"Cookie had a computer question. After you help him,

you take care of your woman."

I stood and forced myself not to slam the door behind me. Hawk was a pain in the ass, and not the good kind like Dani. The 'needed to be taken out back and beat to death' kind.

I found Cookie in the alcove behind the pool table. Sometimes the older kids worked on homework after school or in the rare case of a club lockdown. Cookie was sitting at the one facing the side window and looked about ready to blow a gasket.

"What's up?" I asked.

"Fuckin' virus," Cookie answered.

I shoved the older man aside and went about diagnosing the issue. "Who was last on this?"

"Dirk's kid."

Matthew was fifteen and already a hell-raiser. I shook my head. "Well, Matt's been havin' a little fun. He's downloaded some sketchy porn."

"I thought you did somethin' so the kids couldn't get to it."

"I did, but I didn't go all out. Most kids will get up against the security and not know how to get around it. Matt's figured it out."

"Little shit."

I chuckled. "I'm gonna have to wipe everything and reinstall, but it'll take me a while." I unhooked the computer from the monitor and pulled it from under the table. "Have one of the recruits bring this to my place. I'll upgrade the other computers now and fix this before church."

Cookie nodded and went off to find someone to courier the computer to my place. After I put protection software on the rest of the kids' computers, I took off for home, hoping to get some time with Dani before we had to leave for her parents' place.

I walked into my condo to find Payton and Macey sitting at my kitchen island laughing at something Dani had just said. Dani handed Macey a glass of water and smiled over at me. I tried to keep the disappointment off my face at finding Dani up and clothed. She'd pulled her hair back into a ponytail and wore her sex glasses, and she looked adorable.

"Hi, honey," she said.

"Hey, babe." I closed the door. "Mace, Payton. Good to see you again."

I made my way to Dani and leaned down to kiss her.

She stroked my cheek. "Get everything sorted?"

I grinned. "Kind of. You call your mom?"

Dani nodded. "Yep. All set."

"This is our cue to leave you two," Macey said.

"Uh, yeah," Payton added.

"You don't need to rush off," Dani countered.

"See, that's where you're wrong." Macey giggled. "He has the same look on his face that Dallas gets when he wants to be alone with me."

"And, not that I'm an expert because I have no one who gives a damn, but I see it too," Payton retorted.

"You are ridiculous," Macey said.

"But I'm right," Payton added.

Macey shook her head and then focused on Dani again. "Well, we're gonna let you kids be alone."

I chuckled. "Smart women."

"Booker," Dani admonished.

"What? It's true. I do want alone time with you."

Dani shook her head and pushed away from me. "I'll walk you out."

I grabbed a beer and flopped onto the sofa. I heard Payton and Macey still arguing as they left, and I thought they'd be perfect for some television sitcom. They were hilarious.

I dropped my head back when Dani stood behind me and leaned down to kiss me, our faces upside down. "How was your meeting?"

"Everyone's on the same page for the moment." I took her hand and tugged her around in front of me, pulling her onto my lap and setting my beer aside, so I could wrap my arms around her. "What did you think of Macey and Payton?"

"They're really sweet." Dani smiled. "They're also gorgeous."

"Are they?"

"Nice save." Dani ran her fingers through my hair. "What's the look Macey was talking about?"

"I don't think I gave a look," I said. "But I had hoped you'd still be naked and in bed."

"At three o'clock in the afternoon?"

"Yes."

Dani laughed. "Are you suggesting that I just spend my days naked and in bed, awaiting you to service me whenever you require sex?"

I couldn't stop a wide grin. "Is that an option?"

She leaned down and kissed me. "I'm open to negotiations."

I drew in a quick breath. "What time do we need to be at your parents' place?"

"Six."

I kept her in my arms as I rose to my feet. "Let's start negotiating."

Dani giggled, and I carried her to the bedroom.

* * *

Danielle

I arched my back trying to get closer, but Austin gripped my waist and held me still. I let out a frustrated groan and his chuckle irked me further. I was on my hands and knees, Austin kneeling behind me and he was taking his sweet time making me come.

"Greedy," he whispered as he slid into me again...

slowly.

"Honey," I rasped. "Harder."

He reached between my legs with one hand and fingered my clit, while rolling a nipple with the other, then he slid his hand to my waist and anchored me. "Up, baby."

I sat up and he adjusted me so that I was straddling him backwards, his chest to my back. This position drove him deeper into me and I dropped my head back onto his shoulder. "Austin," I whispered.

"You okay?"

"I can't get close enough."

He laid his hand on mine at my stomach and linked our fingers together. Guiding our hands between my legs, he kissed my neck. "Touch yourself, baby."

"Um…"

"Want me to show you?"

I nodded and he laid his hand over mine again. As he helped me raise and lower my body onto him, the combination of him inside of me and both our hands working my clit, I nearly collapsed when my orgasm hit. Austin rolled me onto my back and slid back inside of me, surging in faster and faster until I felt the pulse of his climax and found myself coming again despite the fact I was so wiped out.

I wrapped my arms around his shoulders and started to giggle.

He leaned up on his arms and smiled down at me. "I'm glad my love-making is comical."

"I just came six times in less than an hour and was pretty much expecting you to do your thing while I lay there. But then I freakin' came again, and I have no idea how I could possibly find the strength to not have it completely kill me, so yeah, I'm a little punchy."

He chuckled. "My job is done."

I smiled and stroked his neck. "If my parents ask why I'm walking funny, I need a cover story."

Austin rolled off me and laughed. "Running injury?"

I snorted. "You need to know something about me. I don't run. Even when being chased. They can just have me."

"We'll figure something out." He slid off the bed and headed to the bathroom while I tried to maneuver my body of jelly under the covers. I was suddenly freezing.

Austin returned and climbed in beside me. "Doctor this week, yeah?"

"If I can get in, yes."

He pulled me up against him. "We can always go to a clinic together. I'll get tested so you don't have to worry, and you can get on the pill."

I rolled to face him. "Would there be any reason for me *to* worry?"

"I'm not a monk, babe."

"I know," I said. "But how long has it been since you've been with anyone?"

"I plead the fifth."

"Why?" I asked slowly.

"Because it hasn't been as long as you would probably like."

"Just tell me."

"About two weeks," he said.

"What? Seriously?" I sat up. "Just a few days before you met me you were in a relationship?"

He shook his head and tugged me onto his chest.

"Hook up?" I asked.

"Yeah, babe. Had a few of those."

"How many is a few?"

"You probably don't want to know," he admitted.

I bit my lip. "Who was the last one?"

"You probably don't want to know that either."

I pushed off of him and sat up on my knees. "Why don't I want to know that?"

He dragged his hands down his face.

"Austin?" I pressed.

"Fuck," he whispered. "Tiff."

I let out a shocked squeal. "Tiff? As in the biker slut who was giving me the stink eye? That *Tiff*?"

"Yeah."

"Ohmigod." I scrambled off the bed and made a run for the bathroom, my stomach suddenly roiling. I couldn't believe how sick I felt, and my stomach continued to rebel even after I'd emptied everything in it.

"Babe?" Austin called from behind the locked door.

"Go away."

"Let me in."

"No," I grumbled. "I'm dying. You shouldn't have to watch it."

"You're actually sick?"

I reached up and unlocked the door. "As opposed to?"

He peeked in. "I thought you were just upset."

"Well, I'm that too."

"I'm so sorry, baby." He hunkered down beside me and pulled my hair away from my face. "You're burning up."

"Bonus."

"I'm gonna run the bath." He rose to his feet. "Let's get that fever down."

I stayed plastered against the toilet, buck naked, as my man filled the tub, grabbed towels, and then helped me off the floor and into the bath... also buck naked. I would have laughed had I not been so pathetically ill.

I dropped my head back against the rim of the tub and sighed. The warm water covered me all the way to my neck and it was divine.

"Dani?"

"Hmm," I mumbled.

"I'm gonna call your brother, yeah?"

"Why?" I opened my eyes and frowned. He'd pulled on pajama bottoms and that kind of made me sad.

"Because you're way too sick to go tonight, but I still need to talk to him."

"Oh, right." I closed my eyes again. "'K."

I vaguely registered his voice as he called my brother, but my body felt like lead and I didn't even have the energy to listen.

"Babe?"

"Mmm?" Austin's cool hand fluttered across my forehead.

"Wake up, baby. Gonna get you dried off and back into bed."

"Can't move."

I groaned when I heard the clunk of the drain being opened and the water whooshing down the drain.

"Okay, baby, let's get you up."

I swallowed, my throat dry and rough. "No."

"You're gonna freeze if we don't get you into bed."

I forced my eyes open and frowned. "I don't care."

Austin chuckled as his hands went under my armpits and he lifted me onto shaky legs, wrapping a huge towel around my body and scooping me from the tub. He sat me on a chair in front of the mirror and gently brushed out my hair. Since I could barely keep my eyes open, he secured the mass with a scrunchy and then helped me back into bed.

I crawled under the sheets and sighed as the coolness of the pillowcase connected with my cheek.

"I'll be back to check on you in a bit."

"'K," I whispered, and passed out.

FIFTEEN

Booker

LLIOT HARRIS ARRIVED at five o'clock, his countenance guarded, but not rude, and I ushered him into the great room. "Can I get you a beer?"

"I'd actually like to see my sister," he said.

"Let me see if she's awake."

"I want to see her even if she isn't."

I nodded. "Follow me."

I led Elliot down the hall to the master bedroom and slid the door open partially. Dani was lying on her back, her hair had come loose from the tie and fanned out over her face, and she was naked from the waist up.

"Give me a sec," I said, and stepped into the room, pulling the covers back up her body.

She groaned and tried to push them down again.

"Dani, your brother's here. He wants to see you."

"Go away," she grumbled.

I slid her hair from her face. "Baby, Elliot's here."

She sat up so quickly, she nearly collided with me. "Ell?"

"I'm here, Dani," Elliot called through the door.

"Don't come in. I'm naked."

I shook my head.

"Why the hell are you naked?" Elliot called.

"Why the hell do you *think* I'm naked?" she retorted.

"Danielle," I whispered.

"What? I've been puking my guts out and miserable, and my brother starts getting all brotherly. It's frickin' annoying." Dani frowned. "Elliot, I'm fine. I have not been kidnapped, I'm not being held against my will, and Austin's only partially a mad-man."

"I'll wait in the other room," Elliot said.

"Good choice, brother of mine," she called.

"You're feeling better," I observed.

Dani nodded, pulling the sheet around her. "Why's my brother here?"

"He came to talk."

"I'll get dressed, then."

I shook my head. "You need to rest."

"I feel great," she said, and promptly began coughing.

"Babe."

"I'm telling you, I feel great. It's all good, honey."

"Probably a burst of energy before the crash."

"Then let me use this burst of energy to see my brother."

I smiled. "You're making it really hard for me to take care of you."

Dani rolled her eyes. "Word of warning, I'm the *worst* patient on earth. Best to learn that now."

"I'll find you something warm and you can get

153

dressed." I rose to my feet. "One of the recruits dropped off a few things—"

"What kinds of things?"

I smiled. "Meds and soup."

Dani looked disappointed. "Oh."

"Expecting something else?"

"I was just dreaming about cheesecake. No big deal."

I laughed. "You were dreaming of cheesecake?"

She licked her lips. "I was eating it off of you."

"Fuck, baby," I whispered, sitting on the bed again. "You can't say shit like that."

Dani giggled. "Why not?"

"One, you're sick as a dog, and two, your brother's here." I grinned. "Wait until you're well and I can do something about it."

"But watching you squirm's kind of fun for me. Especially right now."

"Why especially?"

"Oh, I don't know... maybe because of Tiff."

I sighed. "We'll talk about that later."

"Yes, we definitely will."

"I'll grab you something warm to put on."

"Just grab my bag for me, honey, I can take care of the rest."

"You sure?"

Dani nodded. "I've been sick before and had to deal with it alone, so yes, I'm sure. I'll be out in a minute."

"If your fever doesn't go down, back to bed."

"Yes, mom," she retorted.

I chuckled, kissed her forehead, and retrieved her bag for her before leaving and joining Elliot in the great room.

* * *

Danielle

I watched Austin leave the room and then stared at my

suitcase on the bed. I was spinning emotionally, but I also felt like I was going to die a slow painful death. I chose to pick my battles, and getting the information about Tiff and her relationship with Austin had to be low on the priority list right now.

I climbed off the mattress, my movements stilted and slow as every part of my body ached, and yet, I still had copious amounts of energy. I found clean underwear, sweats, a T-shirt, and a pair of thick socks. I tried to put the socks on, but bending made my head spin, so I took a minute to brush out my hair, pile it on the top of my head again, and brush my teeth.

I padded out of the bedroom and heard the low cadence of male voices as I neared the great room. I exited the mouth of the hallway and the voices stopped. Both my brother and Austin rose to their feet, but it was Austin who walked to me and frowned. "Why don't you have socks on?"

I held the ball up. "Bending over kind of makes me dizzy."

Austin smiled and whispered, "If you're doing it right, it does."

I giggled.

"Come sit down. I'll help," he said, and pulled me to the sofa. Once he'd slid my socks on for me, he headed into the kitchen. "Tea, babe?"

I nodded. "Yes, please."

While Austin made my tea, my brother studied me.

"What, Ell?"

"You really like this guy."

I smiled. "He's amazing."

"Do you know what's going on?"

I nodded. "He told me everything. Are you worried?"

Elliot frowned. "Honestly? Yeah. I knew Steven was an asshole, I just didn't realize he was an evil one as well."

"Austin found my money."

155

"He mentioned that."

"He seems to think he can get it back for me, but he wants to wait it out a bit." I settled my head in my palm, my energy fading. "I'm nervous Steven will hide the money again."

Elliot shook his head. "I think he's too arrogant to believe he'll ever actually get caught."

"There is that," I agreed. "Why would Dad buy policies on us, do you think?"

"He did it right when he became chief." Elliot sipped his beer. "Do you remember Gene Rivers?"

"Dad's old friend from high school?"

Elliot nodded. "Yeah, he's the one who sold him the policy."

"But he died ten years ago."

"I know, but his son Bobby took over his insurance business. Guess who's Bobby's brother-in-law?"

I shrugged.

"Steven."

"What?" I squeaked.

"Steven's sister is married to Bobby."

"Wow," I whispered.

When Steven and I had met and started dating, he'd said his family lived out of state… Vermont to be exact, and it would be impossible for us to meet right away. He'd made a big show… all lies… of "planning" a trip over Thanksgiving, but he'd walked away with all my money a week before the big holiday and I hadn't seen or heard from him again. His phone was a burner that he'd destroyed and I'd found out the last name he'd given me was a fake. He'd said it was Arnold, but my sister had uncovered the truth. Unfortunately, not soon enough to find all of my money. She was only able to find the credit card fraud and that's ultimately what he was prosecuted for.

"This is bigger than we originally thought," Elliot said.

"Sounds like it." I yawned. "Sorry."

"I think you should go back to bed," Austin said, and set a mug of hot tea on the table beside me.

"Nope, I'm good," I said right before a coughing fit.

He frowned, handing me some cold meds and a glass of water. "Take these."

I did as he instructed and wrapped my hands around the mug of tea, sipping it carefully, the heat of the liquid soothing my sore throat. Austin sat beside me and I carefully folded myself into his side, trying not to spill my tea. He wrapped an arm around me and gave me a gentle squeeze.

"What does your father say about all of this?" Austin asked.

"I haven't spoken to him at length," Elliot said. "We'll talk more tonight. But he's gathering all the paperwork he has on file and I'm going to talk to my brother-in-law at length about how to best protect the family. Emily's not an easy mark."

"She's kind of a gun-carrying, badass, with a black belt, so she can defend herself," I piped in.

Elliot nodded. "But that doesn't mean Mitch isn't gonna want to get in on this. He'll also have a game plan."

I wrinkled my nose. "Yeah, I get it. It's all alpha male all the time in her world."

Elliot chuckled. "Shocking that you've found one of your own."

I smiled up at Austin. "Austin's not an alpha male. He's totally meek and easy to deal with. I make all of my own decisions and he just lets me do whatever I feel is best. Why, he tells me everything that's going on in his life, down to the minute detail and he never makes a move on anything without first discussing it with me. He's the best boyfriend ever." I yawned, suddenly finding my eyes difficult to keep open. "I can't seem to stay awake."

"That's because I gave you the nighttime cold meds," Austin revealed.

"What?" I blinked up at him.

Elliot laughed. "You were saying, little sister?"

Austin smiled and took my mug from me. "You're gonna lose your fight to stay awake soon, baby. Just remember that I'm the best boyfriend ever."

"I hate you so bad right now."

"I know. Sleep, sweetheart."

I did.

* * *

I woke up to an empty bed, but feeling a lot better than I had earlier. Having missed a call from Kim and wanting to thank her, I called her back.

"Hey, lady, how are you?" she asked.

I wrinkled my nose. "Sick, actually."

"Yuck. Sorry."

"No problem. Austin's taking care of me. Thanks for getting all that stuff for me. And Mack. I should probably thank him too."

"Oh, he wasn't the one who took me to your place."

"He wasn't? Who was?" I asked and Kim sighed...actually school-girl sighed. "Kimmie?"

"One of the other bikers did. His name's Knight and holy shit, Dani, he's delicious."

"Oh, really?" I grinned. "Are you working your magic?"

She groaned. "He's really young, Dani. I don't know that I *can* work my magic. I might kill him."

I laughed. "How young is really young?"

"I think he's five years younger than me."

"That's still legal, Kim. He's even old enough to drink," I retorted.

"Yeah, but he seems like a good guy. And you know my life isn't sunshine and roses."

"Kimberly Church, you're an amazing woman," I pressed. "The rest is just circumstances because your parents are assholes."

"Amen to that," she said. "He's going to be a vet."

"Really?"

"Yeah. He's into horses too."

"Babe, you realize you're describing the perfect man for you here."

"Possibly."

"Honey, there's no pressure here. Get to know him. I'll talk to Austin about him...get his story."

"If you do that, swear your man to secrecy."

"I will." I started to cough and pulled the phone away from my face. "I should probably go," I said, once I could speak again. "Thanks again for grabbing my stuff."

"No problem. I'll call you later this week."

"Okay. And I'll let you know what Austin says."

"Thanks."

We hung up and I crawled back under the covers.

* * *

Wednesday night I was back at my place and trying to find the will to walk from the living room to the kitchen for some kind of food. It was my first day back at work and I was still a little under the weather, but I always felt guilty taking sick time because I missed my kids. Plus, I always seemed to be missing a stapler when I had to put in for a sub.

Austin was at "church," which he explained meant club meeting, so I was on my own for the moment. Well, alone meaning I had a recruit on me. Buzz was currently sitting in his truck downstairs watching my door. Austin was still concerned there was a threat to me, but since my sleep was a major priority to me, I wanted to be close to school so I didn't have to wake up as early in the morning. Hence the decision to let me be back at my place with the caveat of having someone watch me.

Depending on how late the meeting went, I may or

may not see Austin, and since I didn't think I could find enough energy to care one way or the other, I vegged under a blanket with HGTV on low volume.

My phone buzzed and I answered it without looking at the screen. "Hello?"

"You sound terrible," Kim said.

"I know. But I really do feel better. Just tired from wrangling five-year-olds."

"I bet."

"What's up? I kind of miss your face."

"Me too," she said. "That's what I'm calling about. I don't have to work tomorrow night, so I wanted to see if you wanted to go shopping with me. Maybe grab dinner after?"

"Yes, please," I answered immediately.

"We'll make it an early night so you can get your beauty sleep, but why don't I pick you up at five and we'll head to the mall."

"Perfect."

"No conflict with your man?"

"I see him every day, Kimmie. You I get when I get you, so you're the priority."

She laughed. "That's why you're my favorite. Okay, gotta get back to work. See you tomorrow."

"'Bye." I hung up and set my phone on the coffee table.

I heard the locks in my front door turn and then Austin was walking into the room. He frowned as he sat on the coffee table facing me. "You still sick?"

"Just tired. Why are you here so early?"

"Not a whole lot of business. It only took an hour."

I smiled. "I like it when you're early."

He leaned down and kissed me quickly. "Did you eat?"

"I haven't left the sofa since I got home."

Austin stroked my cheek. "You hungry?"

I nodded. "Starved."

"How hungry?"

"I could eat a cow."

"Okay, I'll run and grab burgers."

"My hero." I grinned up at him. "Onion rings too, please."

He rose to his feet. "You got it."

After he left, I took a few minutes to freshen up a little and then resumed my place on the sofa. The tickle of his stubble woke me, and I smiled as I opened my eyes. "You were quick."

He chuckled. "Been back for almost an hour."

I frowned. "Really? Why didn't you wake me?"

"You needed to sleep. Come eat. Then you should go to bed."

"Are you staying?"

"Yeah, baby, I'm staying."

I smiled again and forced myself to get off the sofa and eat. "What do you think of Knight?"

"Why?" he asked in suspicion.

"Because Kim likes him, but you can't tell him that."

"Not in junior high, Dani, I can guarantee this conversation won't leave the room."

I smiled. "So?"

"Knight's a good guy. Don't know him as well as his brother, Ace, but he seems cool. Knight works at *Blush* when he's not in vet school. He kinda keeps to himself, but he's super tight with his family."

"How old is he?"

"I don't know, Dani. We don't sit around and do each other's nails."

I rolled my eyes. "Well, then what good are you to me?"

"If you'd rather I get personal information from Knight than eat your pussy and make you come, let me know, baby. But that's kind of a deal breaker for me, 'cause I'm not really interested in *not* eatin' your pussy and makin' you come."

I shivered. "Why do you have to make everything sound sexy?"

He laughed. "It's my gift."

"Apparently." I took another bite of my burger and swallowed. "So, what *do* you know about Knight?"

"He's hard workin', his brother's FBI, but we don't hold that against him."

"Wait. His brother's FBI, but you freaked out that my brother's a detective? How does that work?" I challenged.

"Freak out's a little melodramatic, don't you think?"

"Is it?"

"Baby, if I was worried about your brother, you and I wouldn't be together."

"Liar," I retorted. "You locked onto me and I didn't have a lot of choice in the matter."

He raised an eyebrow. "Someone's sassy."

I smiled. "I have to be to keep up with you."

He leaned forward and kissed me, despite my burger breath. "I like you sassy."

"Noted. Now more about Knight, please."

"That's all I know. Hard worker, good guy, obviously an animal lover since he's gonna be a vet. Big horse guy I think. Owns a bunch of 'em."

"So if I were to encourage my best friend to go for it, there would be no ramifications in doing so as far as you know?"

"No ramifications that I'm aware of. All our members go through background checks, and he's one of the truly clean ones. Not even a speeding ticket."

"Hmm," I mused.

"Am I done? Can I eat now?"

I grinned. "Yeah. Maybe later, you can have dessert."

He kissed me again. "Lookin' forward to it."

I managed to finish my food, but could barely keep my eyes open, so I went to bed without Austin, but woke in the night and found him curled around me. There was nothing better in the world than having him close to me. It was something I was quickly getting used to, and I loved every minute of it.

* * *

The next evening, Kim picked me up at five as promised and we headed into Portland to shop. We decided to hit the stores at Jantzen Beach since it was just over the bridge from Vancouver and we could take advantage of no sales tax.

"How long's your muscle going to be around?" she asked.

I glanced behind her and smiled at Train who was far enough behind us to not hear our conversation, but kept me within his sights at all time.

"Until Austin feels this stupid threat is no longer a threat," I said.

"It's weird, but I kind of like that he's protective."

"Yeah, he's both protective *and* weird." I smiled. "He has officially approved Knight."

"What?"

"Austin says Knight's a really good guy and doesn't even have a speeding ticket. He said if you want him, go for it."

"*I* never said I wanted him," Kim countered.

I raised an eyebrow. "He's the first guy in…ever you've even looked at twice. Of course you want him."

"Dani."

"Okay, I'm hearing your 'Dani lay off it' tone, and I will. Just know that I love you and support you whatever you decide to do."

"Thanks."

We strolled through my favorite discount megastore, not really looking for anything in particular, but coming across something that jogged my memory a bit. I grabbed a package of white thigh highs and then headed to the accessories department.

"I'm not going to ask," Kim said with a giggle. "But I'm so glad you're finding your sex kitten side."

I blushed, but managed to keep my head up. "What else should I get?"

"Seriously?" Kim asked, her expression one of excitement.

"Load me up, baby."

Kim clapped her hands and took control of the shopping cart. By the time we waded through the check-out line, I had another pair of thigh-highs, black fishnet this time, three bra and matching panty sets, two strands of faux pearls, and some personal products that apparently made your body feel amazing when applied... they were also edible. I'm pretty sure the cashier blushed almost as red as I did, but she didn't comment and I was grateful. Train was already out front smoking a cigarette, so, far enough away that he couldn't see my purchases.

We decided to head over the bridge for dinner and made our way to Wild Fin, a kickass restaurant and bar on the Columbia River that was a personal favorite of ours.

We sat at a table that gave us a perfect view of the water and ordered margaritas and calamari, and then sat back and looked at the menu. I ordered a burger for Train and asked the waitress to take it to him in his car.

"Tell me about your night with Mack," I said. "I mean, where did you go before you were swept off your feet by Knight."

Kim smiled and closed her menu. "He took me to a honky tonk."

"Shut up. You hate country."

Kim wrinkled her nose. "I know. The club had a room in the back, so they played some great rock stuff and we got to avoid the country."

"Phew," I said, sweeping my hand across my forehead.

"Did he try to get you into bed?"

"Not even once," she said. "We did talk about it though, 'cause, damn, he's hot. But we decided that since we'd probably have to see each other on a regular basis if this thing with our two best friends became permanent, it was best to keep it platonic. Nice guy."

I nodded. "Doesn't talk much, but neither does Austin when he's with his brothers. At least, he doesn't talk about anything of importance. We have our in-depth life-altering conversations in bed."

"Those are the best kind."

I shrugged. "I wouldn't know."

"True, but it sounds like you have a good one now, even if he's kind of bossy."

I snorted. "Bossy doesn't even begin."

"Mack seems like that too. Knight was a lot more laid back and he opened the door and showed me that chivalry isn't entirely dead, even amongst the bad-ass motorcycle club sect."

I snorted. "You're not wrong."

"So, have you and Austin exchanged keys?"

"Yes." I looked at my watch. "He's probably at my place already. We try to spend weeknights at my place, weekends at his."

"You said his place is amazing."

"It's gorgeous. I'll suggest dinner sometime soon. I'll cook. Maybe Knight can come as well."

"Don't," Kim said. "Just let that one lie. If you want to invite Mack, that's good, okay?"

"Okay, honey. I get it."

We caught up on what we hadn't covered... it was rare we didn't talk at least every other day, and if we had something to share, we never waited.

I arrived home to find Booker's bike parked in front and a thrill shot down my spine as I hugged Kim, grabbed my purchases, and headed upstairs to my apartment. I waved to Kim as she pulled out of my parking lot.

"Want help, Dani?" Train called.

"Nah, I'm good."

"Thanks for the burger, by the way."

I grinned. "You're welcome." Dropping an armload of bags on the ground, I unlocked my door and pushed it open. "Austin, are you close?"

"Yeah," he called, and then he was walking toward me.

"I need some help."

"Looks like it." He chuckled, leaned down to kiss me, and took my burdens from me. "Did you leave anything in the store?"

"Not much," I retorted. "Can you dump everything on my mattress and then leave me alone for a bit, please? I have a surprise for you."

"As long as it ends with us in bed, sure thing."

I grinned. "I think it will start with us there."

"Even better." He dumped the bags on my bed and left me to do my thing.

I slid on the white lacy thigh-highs, a pair of white lace panties, and the pearls. I pulled on my robe and then headed into the living room.

Austin's eyes were glued to the television, but he focused on me with a curious smile. "So?" I opened my robe and he hissed. "Fuck me, baby."

I giggled. "That's the plan."

He was off the couch in less than a second and then my robe was yanked from my shoulders, and I was lifted and carried to the bed. He didn't even wait to get all his clothes off before he tore open a condom packet and slid my panties aside so he could slip inside of me.

I gasped, his girth filling me without warning.

"You okay?" he asked.

"Yes." I grinned. "Harder."

He braced his arm on the bed beside me and pushed

my leg up to my chest. It left me open and exposed in a way that made me hot, but what made me hotter was the fact that he held me so tight I had no control over that leg... other than to push against his hand, which assisted in him going deeper. I dropped my head back, arching my chest and within seconds screamed his name as my orgasm hit.

He surged forward a few more times and then shuddered as he collapsed on top of me. I wrapped my arms around his shoulders and kissed his temple. "I forgot the glasses."

He dropped his forehead to mine. "Huh?"

"I still have my contacts in."

Austin laughed. "That's okay. We'll do it again and you can take them out."

"So, this works for you, then?"

"Yeah, babe. It fuckin' works."

"I can't wait to show you what else I have, then."

He met my eyes. "You have more?"

"I do. But you'll just have to wait for those. Can't show you all my secrets at once."

"Yeah, babe, you can."

I giggled. "You need to learn patience. Consider me your teacher."

"As long as you're *sexy* dirty teacher, you got it."

"Whatever you want, honey."

He kissed my neck, then my lips and smiled. "Love you, babe."

"Love you too." I stroked his cheek. "So... can you go get naked now? I'd like to do that again *with* the glasses."

Austin laughed and did as I requested.

SIXTEEN

Danielle

ANOTHER SATURDAY ROLLED around again, and I was at Austin's for the weekend. It had been almost two weeks since my weekend of death, eight days since my start of the pill and his clear blood test, and our first night with no condoms. I'm pretty sure I was currently dead or in some sex-induced coma. I would never have guessed sex could be any better than it had been.

Tonight was another club get-together, but it would be a strictly family party. No one who wasn't attached to someone was invited. I still had Cassidy bugging me to invite her sometime, so I promised to let her know when the next pig roast was.

For the moment, I was sprawled across Austin, naked and sated, our lovemaking on and off throughout the night. His hand ran absently up and down my back, but when his phone rang, it settled on my bottom with a satisfying gentle smack.

"Yo." Austin's voice went from happy and relaxed to irritated in a matter of seconds. "What the fuck?" He frowned, before unwinding himself from me and leaving the bed.

I watched him leave the room, the sight of his perfect ass almost as satisfying as his front, and took a moment to freshen up. I was standing at the mirror brushing out my hair when Austin slid his hands to my breasts from behind and caught my eye with a grin. "I've figured out what my dream job would be."

"You have?"

He nodded and kissed my shoulder.

"And what would that be?" I asked, setting my brush on the counter.

"Your bra."

I giggled. "It's a heavy job."

He gave my breasts a gentle squeeze. "Seriously, babe. You have the best tits. If I could find a way to preserve them forever, I would."

I dropped my head back onto his shoulder as he worked my nipples with his fingers. "They're at your disposal whenever you need them."

He splayed his palm across my belly as he slid his other hand between my legs. "So fuckin' ready."

I licked my lips and moaned as he fingered my wetness and then slid two fingers inside of me. Keeping his fingers inside of me, he pressed gently on my back. "Brace on the counter, baby."

I leaned forward and did as he directed, smiling as he slid into me from behind. "Lower."

I shivered. "The granite's cold."

"It'll add to the sensation, baby. Trust me."

I touched my breasts to the stone and my breath left my body. He was right. It felt amazing.

"Eyes, Dani."

I met his in the mirror and I was suddenly transported into another world as he never took his gaze from me and still managed to give me an orgasm while I was standing there. God, he was the *master*.

He gripped my hips and pulled out slightly, surging back into me, and braced again as he continued to thrust faster and faster. I dropped my head, my body having a difficult time staying upright.

"Eyes," Austin demanded, and I met his again.

His hand slid to my clit again and I cried out as my orgasm hit me. He wasn't far behind and covered my back with his body as he pulsed inside of me.

"Can't breathe," I rasped.

He stood immediately and slid out of me. "Sorry, baby."

I stayed braced on the counter, my shaky arms the only thing keeping me upright, as he wrapped his arms around me again. "Bed."

"I can't move."

He grinned. "I'll help you."

I giggled as we climbed back into the bed and faced each other, heads on our own pillows. "Who was on the phone?"

Austin frowned. "Annie."

"Bad news?"

"She's having trouble with her old man."

I slid my hand under my cheek. "What kind of trouble?"

"He can be a dick."

I studied him. He was holding back and I was debating on how far I'd push him. I decided, pretty damn far. "What aren't you telling me?"

He flopped onto his back and dragged his hands down his face. "She fuckin' called Hawk."

"What do you mean?"

"To help. She called him before me."

"What is your deal with Hawk?" I asked.

"He was our brother... sort of."

"Another foster kid?"

Austin shook his head. "No, he's the real son of our foster parents."

I scooted closer to him, his arm coming automatically around me as I slipped mine across his waist. "What happened?"

"He put Annie in danger, is what happened."

I leaned up on his chest and gripped his chin. "I swear to *God*, Austin, if you don't start giving me detailed information, I'm going to hurt you."

He sighed. "Sorry. I just hate revisiting this shit."

"Well, you either tell me what's going on with you, or you shut up about it," I said, leaning down to kiss him quickly. "I'm a woman, Austin. You can't throw out partial information without my mind running rampant and making up all manner of stories, probably way worse than you could ever imagine. Either you put me out of my misery or you...," I met his eyes and shook my head, "...actually, no. At this point, you just need to fill me in.

Austin laid his hand on my bottom and gave it a gentle squeeze. "Bottom line, he knocked Annie up and then forced her to get an abortion, which was done by a hack, so she started to bleed uncontrollably. She nearly died."

I gasped. "What? Seriously? Why are you in a club with him, then?"

"We were already in when it all went down," he said. "Then, when she admitted his father had been messin' with her, he said nothing. Did nothing. Didn't defend her, didn't testify against his father, nothin'. Fuckin' bastard."

"Weren't you all just kids though, honey? Maybe he

171

didn't have a whole lot of choice."

"We were nineteen, Dani. He was a little older, but not much."

Because I knew this was a hot-button issue for Austin, I chose not to point out that being nineteen didn't really mean much when it came to the difference between being an adult or a child. "What does Annie say about all of this? She obviously doesn't have the animosity toward Hawk that you do."

"She doesn't say anything. She refuses to talk to me about it," he spat out. "Says I'm a loose cannon and can't be trusted not to go off on anyone 'I deem a threat to those I love.'" His body locked and he scowled. "She didn't trust me, but she had no fuckin' problem trusting the bastard who nearly killed her."

I kissed his neck. His sister wasn't wrong when it came to his need to protect. "Sorry, honey."

"Just give him a wide berth tonight, yeah?"

"If that's what you want, yes. But does that fall to Lily too? Because I kind of adore that little girl."

He rolled me onto my back and raised an eyebrow. "I'd be a total dick if I said to keep away from her, huh?"

I nodded. "Total."

"So, what if I said that you should only talk to her if she seeks you out?"

"Then you'd only be half a dick."

"Hmm."

"What?"

"I'm trying to figure out if I can live with that," he retorted.

"You can't." I slid my hand down to grip his cock. "Believe me. I require all of it to stay right where it is."

"Just stick close to me, baby. Avoid him, yeah?"

"I'm a big girl, Austin. Hawk doesn't scare me." I kissed his chin. "Neither do you."

"Really?"

"Really."

He grinned and slid down my body, kneeling between my legs. "What does scare you, babe?"

"Oh, I don't know... heights, spiders, the zombie apocalypse..."

He spread my legs and kissed my inner knee. "What about...?" He kissed my thigh, then gave a gentle suck on my clit. "This."

I squirmed. "That doesn't scare me," I said, a little confused.

"What if I never did this again?" Another suck.

I raised my head to look down my body. "Are you saying that if I don't keep away from Hawk, you won't ever do that to me again?"

He shrugged and I pushed away from him.

"Babe."

"You know how we have the nothing rule?" I snapped.

He sighed, but didn't acknowledge the question.

"We're also going to have the no withholding rule."

"I would never actually withhold anything from you, Dani."

"Then don't threaten to." I pulled my knees up to my chin and wrapped my arms around my legs. "If you don't want me to be best buds with Hawk, then I don't have a problem with that. I'm on your side. Always. *However*, I'm an adult and I'm fully capable of making up my own mind on who I choose to associate with, and the bottom line is that his little girl is adorable and sweet, and he is at least part of the reason she's that way. So, I will be distantly polite to Hawk because I'm Team Booker all the way, but I will never ostracize a little girl because of who her father is."

He cocked his head. "Team Booker?"

I forced myself not to smile. "All the way."

He crawled up the bed, tugging my arms from my legs, and settling his chin on my knees. "I'm sorry, baby."

"Thank you," I said, and slid my legs apart. "Now, make it up to me."

He grinned and did as he was told.

SEVENTEEN

Danielle

WE ARRIVED AT the compound earlier than we'd planned. Austin's sister was apparently on her way and he wanted to see her before Hawk could, which meant we got there before six so Austin could convince her to stay with him.

Austin had gone off with Mack and Hatch, and I was in the kitchen with Susie and a couple of the other ladies, including Hatch's sister, Cricket, helping with food. I wasn't there long before a tall, stunningly beautiful Hispanic woman walked in and studied me. She looked a little like Penelope Cruz and she held herself with a confidence I envied. She wore tight, dark jeans, knee-high black motorcycle boots and a black lace cami under a silver blousy top. Her glossy dark hair hung in straight sheets down her back, stopping at her waist, and she had heavy liner and dark red lipstick that worked with her skin coloring.

"Annie!" Cricket exclaimed.

Susie pulled the younger woman in for a motherly hug. "You look hot, girl."

Annie giggled. "Thanks Suz."

"Is Bullet with you?" Cricket asked.

Annie shook her head. "Just me."

"Good for you."

"You must be Dani," Annie said, and hugged me. "Booker won't shut up about you, so I think I'd know you anywhere."

I blushed. "It's nice to meet you, finally."

"Where is my big brother?"

"You didn't see him when you came in?" I asked.

Annie shook her head.

"Maybe he's in his room," I said.

"Let's go see," Annie said, and took my arm. "Be back."

"Take your time," Susie said.

Annie and I walked upstairs and down the hall to Austin's room. I knocked and turned the knob… it gave. His door was usually locked, so I figured he must be in there and pushed it open, my stomach turning at what I saw. Tiffany lay on the bed, naked, as though waiting for him.

Annie hissed. "What the fuck are you doin' here?"

"I'm waiting for Booker. He'll be here any minute." Tiffany faced us, her head in her hand, and gave me a smug look. "What are you doing here?"

Tiffany had what most would consider a kickass body. Long legs emphasized her five-foot-eight slender body, and her large breasts, albeit fake, sat perfectly in the middle of her chest mostly because that's where they were designed to be. She had a belly button ring and was shaved completely… down there. I was reminded that this is what

Austin was used to. Not me with my extra weight and my overly large breasts that often got in the way most days. Not to mention my legs that I'd always referred to as tree stumps. I was short. Really short in comparison to Tiff.

I backed out of the room and Annie followed, pulling the door closed with a slam. "You okay?" she asked.

I shook my head and tried to swallow the bile threatening to spill.

"Dani, my brother does *not* cheat. This can't be what it looks like."

"How would she have gotten in there if he hadn't planned it?" I challenged. "Only a few people have keys."

Before Annie could respond, heavy footsteps sounded in the hallway.

"There you are. Been lookin' everywhere for you," Austin said, and then stopped and frowned. "What's wrong?"

I blinked back tears and bit my lip.

Austin moved Annie out of the way and squeezed my arms. "Babe. What's wrong?"

"Your... um," I swallowed, "whore is waiting for you."

"What the fuck?"

"Tiff," Annie said.

He shook his head. "Not following."

"Tiff is on your bed, naked and ready, Booker." Annie crossed her arms. "She told us she was waiting for you."

"What the hell?" Austin snapped. "I'll deal with this."

He released me, shoved open his door, and closed it behind him. Annie rolled her eyes and pushed the door open again.

"How the fuck did you get in here?" Austin bellowed.

"Buzz let me in," Tiffany answered.

"And why the fuck would he let you in my room, Tiff?"

"I told him I was meeting you here."

"Why would you tell him that?"

177

"Because I figured you'd be happy about it," she said.

"Get the fuck out."

"Baby, I know you miss me," she purred. "What the hell can that little goody two shoes do for you? She probably doesn't even know how to give a decent blow job."

Annie wrapped an arm around my shoulders as I burst into quiet tears. Tiffany was right. I wasn't enough for Austin.

"You're a fuckin' idiot, Tiff," Austin snapped.

"We could share," she offered. "I wouldn't mind. She's pretty in a Little House on the Prairie kind of way. A little chubby, but still kinda pretty."

It was like the woman was in my mind, saying out loud every insecurity I'd ever had. Before I could fully break down, Austin was pushing a very naked Tiff out of the room, his hand wrapped around the back of her neck.

"What the hell, Booker?" she squealed, trying to cover herself with her arms.

With his free hand, he pulled out his cell phone and put it to his ear. "Buzz, get the fuck up here. Now!"

It wasn't long before Buzz was rushing towards us.

"You let this skank in my room?" Austin snapped.

"She said you wanted her to wait for you," Buzz answered.

"On notice, yeah? If she ever shows her face within a hundred miles of anywhere Dogs related, I will ruin her."

Tiffany's face went white. "What?"

"You get me, Buzz?" Austin asked.

"Yeah, Booker. Sorry," he stammered.

"But, it was just a joke," Tiffany rushed to say. "I meant it as a joke. Everyone knows you're with Dani. I wouldn't have done anything."

"One fuckin' night with you and I'll regret it forever," Austin said, his face contorted in rage. "It wasn't even good, but I tried to be respectful anyway. Can't believe I wasted my time on you when just a few days later I was given someone near perfect." He still had his hand wrapped around the back of her neck. "You've gone through pretty much everyone here, Tiff, so you can head on downstairs and see if there are any other takers before you get the fuck out of here for good."

"I'm not going down there naked, Booker," she snapped.

"Why the hell not? You said you'd share. So what makes me so special all of a sudden? You want a three-some so bad, go see if anyone wants to take you up on it. But it's your last chance, Tiff, so make it count, because I see you anywhere near the club, me, or my woman again, you'll find out what I'm like when I'm pissed. Got me?"

She nodded and he shoved her away in disgust.

"What about my clothes?" she asked.

"You wanna play the whore, babe, you don't need clothes."

I covered my mouth with my hand, both liking the way Austin was standing up for me, but also a little sad at another woman's humiliation... even if she did bring it on herself.

"Buzz, no one in my room except me or Dani, yeah?" Austin demanded.

"Yeah, Booker. Sorry."

Austin scowled at Tiff. "What are you waiting for? Fuck off."

She started down the hall, her head bowed, her countenance very different than it had been a few minutes ago. I stood in stunned silence, Annie's arm still around me, and watched as Austin stepped back into his room and emerged holding Tiff's clothes. He shoved them at Buzz and then grabbed my arm and pulled me inside. Annie followed.

He wrapped his arms around me and pulled me against his chest and I couldn't stop myself from crying into his shirt.

"Baby. It's okay," he whispered.

"I thought... I..."

"I know."

"I'm so sorry. I should have trusted you."

"We're still new. Tiffany's a bitch, but she's a smart bitch. She had a fifty-fifty shot of freaking you out enough to mess with your head. I don't think she was ready for the consequences though."

I glanced up at him. "Thank you for giving her back her clothes."

"Baby, there are kids downstairs."

I leaned back with a frown. "So, if it was adults only, you wouldn't have given them back?"

He smiled. "I'm pleading the fifth on that one."

"Probably a good choice." I buried my face back in his chest and let him hold me.

"So you fucked Tiff," Annie murmured

"Don't start," Austin said.

"That's scrapin' the very bottom of the barrel big brother. What the hell?"

"I was drunk and horny. She was there and willin'." My body locked and Austin gave me a gentle squeeze. "But we don't need to go there."

"Ignore her, Dani," Annie said. "She's a total skank who seriously has fucked pretty much everyone in the club, other than a couple of the recruits."

"But that's kind of sad," I said.

"How so?"

"Because when a woman feels insecure enough to sleep around, especially that much, she has bigger issues... like her dad didn't love her enough maybe. I think that's sad."

"Holy shit, Booker," Annie said. "How the hell did you manage to convince this woman to give you a chance? She's obviously too good for you."

"I'm hoping she won't figure that out until after I marry her." He kissed the top of my head. Austin loosened his arms and pulled me to the chair opposite Annie's. He sat down and guided me onto his lap, wrapping an arm tightly around my waist. Because he was so much taller than me and the chair was huge, I was able to settle myself on his chest quite comfortably.

"What's going on with Bullet?" he asked.

"Maybe you should talk about this in private," I said.

Annie waved her hand dismissively. "Honey, if you've got my brother talking marriage, you're already family."

"This is the first I've heard of it," I said.

"Classic Booker," Annie said with a giggle. "Romance is not his forte."

I bit my lip which made Austin chuckle. "She knows."

"He's romantic in his own way," I said.

"Seriously," Annie said. "Saint."

"Yeah, she is." Austin kissed me quickly.

"Stop," I whispered, but I had to admit I was feeling better than before.

"What's going on with Bullet?" Austin asked his sister.

Annie grinned. "Nothing he won't learn from."

"So it's like that," Austin murmured.

"He just needs to miss me a little I think." Annie cocked her head. "Something you'll need to learn, Dani, is when these men get out of line, or start to take you for granted, you need to dish out some lady justice. Keep 'em on a tight leash."

"Shut the hell up, Annie," Austin said with mock irritation.

I giggled. "If I run into issues with this one, I'll call you."

"You will not," Austin said. "You will never have her phone number."

"We'll see," Annie said. "Let's get downstairs. I'm ready to get my drink on."

"You're comin' home with us tonight, right?" Austin asked.

"If you don't mind."

"We don't mind," I said, quickly and climbed off Austin's lap.

Annie and Austin stood, and Austin grabbed my hand. "We'll meet you down there, Annie." She nodded and left the room and Austin pulled me into his arms. "You okay?"

I looped my hands around his neck and smiled. "I will be. I'm sorry I thought the worst."

"I promise, I'll never cheat, baby. If I fuck up so badly you stop loving me and giving me you, then we'll break up, but I won't ever cheat."

"I love you."

"Love you too, babe." He leaned down and kissed me, and it quickly turned heated. Austin laid me down on the bed and, as was his go-to, he slipped his hand under my shirt and pulled down the cup of my bra. His fingers rolled my nipple and I whimpered as I deepened the kiss. I felt a buzzing from his pocket and he broke the kiss with a curse. Rolling onto his back, he answered his phone. "What? Yeah. Okay." He hung up.

I sat up and fixed my bra and shirt.

"Sorry, baby. We'll resume this later," he said and slid off the mattress, pulling me with him.

"Everything okay?"

Austin nodded. "Bullet's here."

"Oh," I said. "Drama?"

He chuckled. "One thing you'll learn about Annie, there's always drama. Come on, let's go have some fun."

I checked my appearance in the mirror and then followed him downstairs. A tiny body collided with my legs from behind and I glanced down to see Lily hugging me.

"Dani, Dani, Dani."

I hunkered down beside her and grinned. "Well, hello pretty girl. How are you?"

Lily jumped up and down. "Daddy said I could stay up and have a cupcake."

"Oh, my goodness! That's so exciting. May I join you for the cupcake?"

She nodded.

"But you have to eat your dinner first, right?"

She nodded again, but her little nose went up in a wrinkle.

I giggled. "Good girl."

I stood again and she slipped her hand in mine as we continued into the great room. We walked in to find a standoff of sorts with Austin, Hawk, Mack, and a tall blond man who was having it out with Annie, however, I didn't miss his devotion to her. He stayed connected to her, kept himself between her and the other men, and they may have been arguing, but I could see a spark of mischief in her expression, which made me think she was very happy to see her man.

"Daddy!" Lily called.

Hawk turned toward me, gave me a look of pleading, and then turned back to the group. I scooped Lily up in my arms and smiled. "Let's go find those cupcakes, huh?"

We walked into the kitchen where Susie met us and waved me to a door at the back of the room. I carried Lily through and saw that a few of the ladies and older kids were playing with the little ones in a well-equipped play-room. I set Lily down and she went straight for the kitchen set. With my shadow occupied, I left the playroom and headed back to the great room.

I noticed Austin's body was stiff, his expression one of rage, and I wondered what had happened between the time I dropped Lily off in the playroom and now. He and Hawk were in the middle of a stare down and Annie had her hands on each of their arms. Bullet stood close to the threesome, but gave his woman a little space.

"You are a fuckin' piece of shit," Austin hissed.

"I learned from the best," Hawk retorted.

Hatch watched them closely but didn't step in…yet.

"What the hell is your problem, Booker?" Annie demanded.

Austin turned his head slowly. "Why are you so eager to forgive him?"

"For *what*?" she demanded.

"For nearly killing you."

"What the hell are you talking about?"

"The doctor!" Austin spat out.

"The abortion?"

"Well, yeah."

"You think Hawk forced me to do it?"

"He fuckin' knocked you up, so yeah!"

"What?" Hawk snapped.

Annie removed her hands and burst out laughing.

"What the fuck, Annie?" Austin demanded.

"Booker. Hawk didn't get me pregnant. Marvin Adams did."

"The center for the Trojans?"

Annie nodded. "Yeah. He was worried about a possible basketball scholarship to Oregon State, so he gave me the money and it went bad. Hawk just happened to be home when I started to hemorrhage. Honey, he took care of me. He's the reason I didn't bleed to death."

Austin glanced at Hawk. Both their bodies were considerably more relaxed.

"This is where all this hostility shit's been coming from?" Hawk asked.

Austin rubbed his forehead. "And the fact you didn't testify against your father… yeah."

"He didn't testify because he didn't need to," Hatch said.

"Meaning?" Austin asked.

Hawk sighed. "I signed an affidavit attached to a detailed account of everything I knew about in terms of what

184

Annie told me, along with what I'd observed. You found the proof, so the attorneys figured pitting me against the bastard might do more harm than good. You know I have nothing to do with him. He's fuckin' dead to me."

"Fuck," Austin rasped.

This was when I moved. I closed the distance between us and wrapped my arms around his waist. Austin settled his hand at the back of my neck, thumbing my pulse.

"Brother, I'm sorry," Austin said to Hawk.

"You're a fuckin' moron," Hawk said, and then laughed. "Fuck me, if I'd known this was what got your panties in a wad, I'd have told you years ago."

Austin cracked a semblance of a smile and then it was done. This feud they'd had for ten years was over. I shook my head. It must be pretty awesome to be a guy some days.

The rest of the night was somewhat uneventful. Food was eaten, booze was consumed, and I finally got to find out if the bed in Austin's room was as comfortable as it seemed. It was.

Especially when I was kneeling between his legs and drawing his cock deep into my mouth, his hands gripping my head. I was quickly figuring out why Kim loved this so much. I gripped the base of him with my hand squeezing gently as I sucked a little harder. I knew I'd hit the mark when Austin began to fuck my mouth, his hips surging up faster and faster.

"Babe," he rasped, and I smiled. I moved my hand in time with my mouth and he groaned. "I'm gonna come."

I kept going.

"Babe, I'm gonna come."

I raised my eyes. "Come," I mumbled, his thickness still filling me.

He did. "Fuck."

I waited until he relaxed and then gave one more suck, kissing the tip of his cock before crawling up his body.

"Ohmigod, that was so fun."

"You lied when you said you'd never done it before."

I giggled. "I totally didn't, but I love you for saying it."

He cupped my cheek. "Baby, I'm not kidding. Best blow job I've ever had."

"You're not just saying that?"

"I'm not just saying that." He pulled me closer and kissed me.

"Beginner's luck?"

"No. I think it's us," he said. "Never been in love before, so it's probably just our perfection as a couple."

I laughed. "And Annie doesn't think you're romantic."

"I'm romantic because it's you."

I sat up and then straddled his hips. "Wanna get romantic again?"

He chuckled. "What did you have in mind?"

"My turn to romance you."

"Romance away, baby."

A more beautiful challenge had never been given, and I turned my beginner's luck into pure unadulterated experience.

EIGHTEEN

Danielle

SUNDAY AFTERNOON, I was standing in Austin's bathroom applying a little lipgloss when he walked into the room, his usual biker uniform nowhere to be seen. He still wore the jeans and cut I loved a little too much, but he had on a long-sleeved, soft T-shirt a deep blue that matched his eyes.

I smiled and tilted my head. "You look unbelievably hot, if not rather conservative."

"Meeting your parents, babe. Want to be respectful."

I slid my hands to his neck. "Love you."

"Love you too." He grinned and kissed me quickly. "Ready?"

I nodded and followed him out of the bedroom and

grabbed my purse. He took my hand as we headed to the garage and opened the truck door for me before climbing in himself. We stayed connected as we drove to my parents' home and it helped calm my excited nerves.

My parents lived in the Felida, a place that used to be filled with farms and homes on large parcels of land. Now it was filled with mini mansions, newer custom homes jammed close together, and some of the higher earning executives in the Portland metro area chose to live here. My parents' home overlooked the river just off Lakeshore. I had been born in this house, as had my brother and sister. But the sad reality was, that unless I got my money back, I'd never be able to afford to live in the exclusive area.

Austin pulled his truck into the driveway and parked. He jogged to my side of the truck and opened the door, pulling me close and kissing me once I stepped out.

"Nervous?" he asked.

"Excited," I said. "You?"

He grinned. "Once I meet your family, it's forever, so, yeah. Excited."

I snorted. "Even if you weren't meeting them, honey, you're kind of stuck with me."

He kissed me again. "Even better."

He opened the back door of the truck cab and grabbed the flowers he'd brought for my mother, the wine I chose for dinner, and then locked up his truck.

I took the wine and linked my fingers with his, tugging him to the door. My parents rarely locked the front door, so I pushed it open and giggled when I found my mom walking towards us. "Have you been watching from the window?"

She laughed. "I won't answer that question."

"Good idea," I said, and pulled Austin forward. "Mom, this is Austin. Austin, this is my mom."

"It's nice to meet you, Mrs. Harris." He handed her the flowers.

"These are beautiful. Thank you." My mom pulled him in for a hug. "You can call me Brenda. Come and meet the rest of our crazy crew."

We followed my mom to the back of the house where the kitchen and great room were filled with my family. Elliot took over the introductions while I joined my sister and mother in the kitchen to help.

"Crap," my mom said. "I'm one stick of butter short."

"I'll run next door and see if Missy can spare one," I offered.

"Thanks, honey, that would be great."

I smiled and made my way to where Austin had made himself comfortable on the sofa, my brother and brother-in-law in a full-on debate about which football team was better, while Austin and my father sipped their beers and watched.

I leaned over him and kissed him. "I'm running next door to grab some butter."

"I'll come with you."

"I'm quite capable to walking a few yards for butter. Stay here and relax."

He smiled up at me and kissed me once more, and I grabbed my jacket and headed outside.

* * *

Booker

Dani had been gone for almost twenty minutes and I was getting anxious. "Dani's been gone a while."

Elliot chuckled. "Missy's probably talking her ear off."

I nodded, but it didn't make me feel better. Five minutes later, I stood and grabbed my jacket. "Where's this Missy person's house?"

"I'll come with you," Elliot offered, and led me from the house.

We walked next door and knocked on the door. An

older woman, probably in her sixties answered the door. "Well, hi there, Elliot."

"Hey, Missy. We're just looking for Dani. Is she still here?"

"Still? She hasn't been here at all, honey."

"Shit," I snapped, and pulled out my cell phone. Dani hadn't taken her phone with her, so I didn't have a trace on her. I called Train, but he didn't answer, so I called Mack.

"Yo," Mack said.

"Dani's missing, and I can't find Train."

"You track her?"

I rubbed my forehead. "Her cell phone, yeah, but she doesn't have it with her."

"We'll find her, brother," Mack promised.

I hung up at the same time Elliot did.

"Got my team on it," Elliot said.

"Mine too," I said.

Elliot nodded.

My phone rang and I saw Train's name pop up. "Where the hell are you?"

"Saw her get pinched, brother. Two guys, black Escalade. They're heading into Gresham."

"I'm on my way. Call me when you have an address."

Train hung up and I made a run for my truck... Elliot followed, jumping into the passenger seat just in time as I reversed out of the driveway. I sped toward Gresham, uncaring I was in my truck with a cop. I needed to find Dani.

Elliot was on his phone the entire time, either filling his father in on what was going on or talking to his partner. He'd also called in a buddy's FBI team who worked out of Portland since they were familiar with Gresham, and the scumbag sect that inhabited parts of it.

Train texted an address in a more rundown area of the city, and I arrived to find several of my brothers... some on their bikes, a couple in trucks... all armed and amped up to fight. I couldn't worry about the fact that my club was about to collide with the law. Right now, I'd do anything to make sure Dani was safe. I grabbed my gun from the glovebox and climbed out of the truck.

A black SUV pulled in behind my truck and Dallas Stone exited, along with another man who I didn't recognize.

"Booker," Dallas said with a nod. "My partner, Brock."

I gave him a chin lift. "Can't touch the club, Dallas."

"Not here to bust the club, Book. Macey likes your girl, so we're here off the record."

I nodded and joined Train. "Where?"

Train nodded toward a blacked out industrial building about a block down from where they were standing. "They went around the back."

I nodded and started toward the building. "Follow me."

* * *

Danielle

I came awake with a start, mostly because my head felt like an ice-pick was jamming itself into my temple. I opened my eyes... well, kind of... one of them didn't seem to want to work, and I looked around. I was in a tiny room, tied to a chair, and my memory flooded back to me.

I had just stepped out of the house and was halfway up my parents' driveway when I was grabbed from behind. I fought as best I could, my self-defense training helping, but ultimately, there were two men and each of them outweighed me by at least a hundred pounds.

What I did manage to do was piss them off, and I remember pain in my ribs and face before I blacked out.

I swallowed and tried to figure out where I was. Austin would come. I knew he would. I didn't know how I knew; I could just feel it in my gut. I took a deep breath, grimacing at the pain in my ribs. Breathing was probably not a good idea right now.

For the moment I was alone, but I didn't know how long that would last. I heard male voices near the door, so I dropped my head and tried to go as limp as possible.

"What the hell do you mean the guy canceled the policy? Fuck you, Bobby. We took this bitch for no reason? Well, then there's no reason to keep her alive."

I tried not to react even though my heart sank into my stomach.

"Yeah. Okay. Well, shit. A mil's not even close to ten, dumbass. You don't take a cut, I don't tell where I got my information. Otherwise, everyone's gonna know who the hell you are." The man chuckled... a low, sardonic, and very creepy chuckle. "How about you fuck off and figure out how to make this right."

I was in a weird enough position that even though I'd managed to open my good eye a sliver, I couldn't see who was speaking. Since it hurt to try, I closed them again.

"Bitch's dad canceled the policy and Bobby forgot to tell us," the man who'd been talking before complained.

"Shit, Ken, what does that mean?"

"Her family's loaded, so Bobby thinks we'll get at least a mil for her," Ken said.

"Fuckin' idiot."

"Yeah, Sal, I'm with you."

"How long we gonna give the parents?"

"Six hours," Ken answered. "Then we kill her."

"You think they can get that much together in six hours?"

"I don't care. She saw us, so either way, she's dead."

They continued to talk, but their voices faded as they walked out of the room, closing the door behind them. I looked up again and tried not to panic. I needed to keep my wits about me and get the hell out of here.

I tested my bindings and discovered the more I moved, the more it hurt. I was tied with plastic zip ties that cut into my skin. Each of my ankles was zip tied to a chair leg and a rope around my waist had me pretty much stuck to the chair. My mouth was covered with what I assumed was probably duct tape, and it didn't budge when I scrunched up my face.

I had no concept of how long I'd been in the room. There was no window, so I couldn't tell how dark it was outside. It was still light when we'd gotten to my parents' place, but the sun was starting to set.

I sighed. I wish I had my phone. I knew Austin had put a tracker on it, but didn't think I'd need it if I was just stepping next door.

I closed my eyes again and succumbed to darkness. I don't know how long I'd been out, but the deafening sound of gunfire had me waking in fright, and then the door to the office flew open and I screamed behind my muzzle.

"Booker! In here," Mack called.

I burst into tears as Mack rushed to my side and cut the bindings on my hands then my feet just as Austin arrived and knelt in front of me.

"Baby." He gently peeled the tape from my mouth and I collapsed in his arms.

"I knew you'd come," I cried. "But did it have to take you so long?"

He lifted me and I whimpered at the pain. Then I passed out.

* * *

I woke to hushed voices and opened my eyes to find Austin's head leaning on my arm, his hand holding mine.

"Dani?" my mother crooned and walked toward me.

Austin stood and leaned over my bed, a tentative smile on his face as he swept my hair from my forehead. "Hi, baby."

"Hi," I rasped and grimaced. My throat was burning. "Water."

Austin nodded and grabbed me a cup and a straw, guiding it to my mouth. I drank deeply and then relaxed back onto the mattress.

My mother squeezed my hand and smiled. "You gave us a scare, baby girl."

I nodded.

"I'm going to let the nurse know you're awake," she said.

I nodded again and she left the room. I reached for Austin, who took my hand and pulled it to his lips. "Fuck me, baby. It took me two hours to get you out."

"That's all?" I asked.

He frowned. "That's a fuckin' long time when I'm scared outta my mind not knowin' if you were okay."

I smiled. "I knew you'd come."

"We're gettin' married."

"We are?"

He nodded. "Tomorrow."

I chuckled, ending on a whimper at the pain in my ribs.

"Sorry, baby. You've got a couple broken ribs."

"I'm okay, honey." I squeezed his hand. "A little beat up, but okay."

I could see the sheen of tears in his eyes, but he turned his head and blinked them away.

My door opened and Macey Stone walked in, her light-blue scrubs crisp and clean. "I'd hoped our second get-together would have been dinner or something, but I guess I'll have to take a rain check."

I smiled. "You're on."

"How's your pain level?" she asked. "From one to ten?"

"About an eight."

Macey nodded and checked the pain pump next to me. She pressed a button on the unit and then handed me a wire and smiled. "Press the red button when it wears off. It'll let you dose yourself every four hours."

"Thanks."

The nurse took my pulse and notated a few things in my chart, before smiling and focusing on me again. "All told, Dani, you were really lucky. I'll let the doc know you're awake and he'll be in shortly."

"Thanks, Macey."

"My pleasure, hon."

She left the room and my entire family flooded inside, along with Kim. Austin stepped back and sat on the bench by the window as my niece and nephew hugged me gently, Amelia talking a hundred miles a minute, a clear indication she'd been concerned about me.

The doctor arrived and ordered everyone out.

"Can Austin stay?" I asked.

"Sure."

My dad shared some secret badass man chin lift with Austin and then my family filed out of the room and Austin stood beside my bed again.

"I'm Dr. Stone," the handsome doctor said.

"Related to Macey?"

"She married my brother," Dr. Stone said. "Lucky bastard."

I smiled.

"Let's have a look at you."

The doctor looked me over and decided that I could go home the next day. They'd keep me overnight for observation, but since my eye-socket was bruised, not broken as they initially had worried, and the ribs would heal on their own, there was no point in keeping me any longer.

He left and my family descended again, staying for close to an hour before Emily forced hers to leave and my mother convinced my dad and Elliot to go as well.

Kim leaned over the bed and kissed my cheek. "Love you, hon. Please no more kidnapping, okay? You totally freaked me out."

I chuckled. "That's a promise."

She smiled, hugged Austin, and then headed out and Austin took his place beside the bed again.

Late that night, Austin and I were finally alone and I scooted over and patted the mattress. "I need you to sleep with me."

He smiled as he climbed beside me. "This is probably against hospital policy."

"Where's my big badass motorcycle man?" I demanded. "Are you telling me you're afraid of hospital security?"

He chuckled and gently settled me on his chest. "I'm more afraid of Macey."

"Ooh, I know, right? She's kind of scary."

"I love you, beautiful."

"Mmm, I love you too." I raised my chin for a gentle kiss and then snuggled close.

"Marrying you in a month, babe."

"What?" I squeaked and looked up at him again.

Austin smiled. "I talked to your dad. It's all set. We're gettin' married by the water in their yard. Small and intimate like."

"Do I have any say in this?"

He shook his head. "You can pick your dress. Otherwise, Emily and Kim have the rest of it under control. They said they know what you want or something."

I sighed. "Yeah, they know."

"Good. It's settled."

"I don't have a ring."

"Got that planned, baby. When you're feelin' better, I'm gonna get romantic."

I laughed. "Seriously?"

"Hell, yeah. Gonna blow your mind."

I closed my eyes and kissed his chest. "Love you, baby."

"Love you too, Dani."

We stayed like this all night. I was restless with pain, but Austin kept track of the time and would dose me every four hours like clockwork, which meant I slept even if he didn't. I couldn't believe how lucky I was to fall in love with the most amazing man on earth, especially after my track record.

I fell asleep knowing I was the luckiest woman alive.

* * *

Booker

I slid the covers up Dani's body and kissed her temple. She was finally asleep, the pain meds and muscle relaxers coursing through her system making her more comfortable. I pulled the door partially closed and headed to my office, phone in hand.

"Hello?" Kim answered.

"Hey. You got time to come hang with Dani for a bit? I have shit to do."

"Sure. I can be there in twenty minutes."

"Thanks, Kim."

I hung up and called Mack.

"Yo."

"You got him?" I asked.

"Yeah, brother. He's here," Mack said. "Prez and Hatch are here too."

"Why?"

"Make sure you don't kill him."

"Fuck." I dragged a hand through my hair. "You got my back they get in the way?"

Mack chuckled. "When don't I?"

"Thanks, brother."

I hung up and slipped my phone into my pocket. I needed to ride today, so I grabbed my leathers from the closet. Kim arrived a few minutes later.

"If she's in pain, she can have painkillers in three hours… everything's on the counter. I don't know how long I'll be, but if you run into any issues, text me."

Kim nodded. "Got it. Do what you gotta do, I've got Dani."

I leaned down and kissed her cheek. "Thanks, babe."

I made it to the club in record time, my thoughts occupied with Dani and the bastard I was about to teach a lesson to. Maybe it was good that Crow and Hatch were there… I was pissed enough to kill him, and I was pretty sure Dani's cop family would back me up.

I walked through the common room, into the kitchen, and down the stairs to the cellar where Mack was waiting.

I closed the door at the bottom of the stairs and made my way to where Steven was zip-tied to a chair… exactly the way Dani had been in the warehouse.

"Remember me?" I asked with a sneer.

Steven's eyes grew wide with fear as he stared up at me.

"I found Dani's money… I also found all of yours." I rolled up my sleeves. "All of this information, including the money you stole are with the FBI. I took the liberty of retrieving Dani's first, with interest from your own stash. Dani's gonna have a perfect little house wherever the hell she wants because she can afford it now."

Steven mumbled behind the duct tape.

"Sorry? Did you say something?" I asked, and slammed my fist into Steven's face. "Oops, sorry. That was a slip… I actually meant to do this." I slammed my fist into his stomach. Steven squealed on a grunt and then tried to draw air in through his nose. "One thing you're gonna find out is what it's like to live under the watchful eye of the NSA."

Steven let out a muffled "Fuck you."

I laughed. "Nah...that's all you, bro. See, I kinda hacked into the homeland security terrorist database and according to your record... did you know you now have a record?"

Steven grunted.

"Yeah, you have a record, and according to your record, you've been stockpiling money to fund a bombing... murder of the president... something like that. So, the government has seized all your assets and you are on the no-fly list, domestic terrorism list, along with several other interesting lists that I didn't even know existed. Bottom line is you can't really walk out your front door without someone knowin' about it. Oh, and by the way... your house has been repo'd... good luck finding a shithole to put a sleeping bag in. You're welcome for that. It's the least I could do. I think it's fitting that you get what you deserve." Steven mumbled again, so I pulled off the tape. "What was that?"

"Why are you doing this?" he asked. "I would have given back the money."

"My woman got taken, asshole. They beat her and threatened to kill her, and even if you weren't directly responsible for that, I found the email from Bobby telling you about the policy and the suggestion to use it in an alternative to your plan. But that wasn't good enough for you. You chose to use her physically and emotionally instead. Which means, you're dealing with me now."

"You won't get away with this!"

"But I already have," I said matter-of-factly.

"Fuck you!" Steven spat.

I laughed and shoved the tape over his mouth again.

For the next hour, I took my time making Steven hurt. I delivered every injury Dani received, and then some, before releasing him in the middle of a park, naked and without ID.

I, on the other hand, headed home, found my woman awake and laughing with her best friend, and I knew she was okay. She loved and was loved and that's all that mattered.

EPILOGUE

Danielle

Two years later…

I STOOD AT the bathroom counter staring down at the little blue stick I'd just peed on. Austin and I had been married for twenty-three months, six days, and nineteen hours, and I'd been feeling nauseous and tired for about a week.

I was alone in the Naito condo that we now shared as a married couple and expected him home any minute. I was officially on dinner duty, but the smell of meat turned my stomach, so I was going to have to figure something else out.

As I waited for the results of my pregnancy test, I

thought back to our blissful engagement, quick marriage, and perfect extended honeymoon. True to his word, he'd gotten romantic and proposed to me in the middle of Portland's Saturday market with most of his club, all of my family, and Kim in attendance. He'd even gotten down on one knee and slipped the biggest frickin' diamond I'd ever seen on my finger.

I stared at it now as I tapped my foot and checked the stick. Nothing.

My ring sparkled back at me, the six-carat diamond and matching diamond wedding band proof that I was married to the hottest guy on the planet.

We'd gotten married in my parents' back yard, and Kim and Emily had outdone themselves. I'd chosen an off-white Vera Wang gown that hugged every curve perfectly and made me feel like a princess. Austin had worn an Armani tux that had literally been made for him, while Mack stood as his best man and Kim stood as my maid of honor.

My father walked me down the aisle, his eyes glistening with tears as he kissed me and told me how proud of me he was, and how happy he and Mom were of my choice. Austin had woven himself so well into my family it was like he'd been there forever.

Our wedding night at the Hotel Monaco in Portland was filled with love, sex, and an envelope holding the money Austin had recovered from my ex. Austin had put it into a secure account in my married name with alerts aplenty should anyone else try to access it but me. Then he'd whisked me off to Maine where we stayed at a tiny little remote cabin by the water and gorged ourselves on fresh crab and lobster. I don't recall getting dressed most of the trip, declaring that naked lobster-fests needed to be a regular occurrence. He'd agreed and we'd spent another sexy week in Maine for our one-year-anniversary.

I was coming up on the end of another school year and trying to decide if I was going to continue teaching or do something else. If this test was positive, it would make my decision easier.

"Babe?" Austin called.

"Bedroom."

I met him in the hallway, the pregnancy test behind my back, and stood on my tiptoes to kiss him. "Hi."

"Hi, baby. You okay?"

"Unbelievably okay."

He chuckled. "Oh yeah?"

I pulled the stick from behind my back and held it up. "You're gonna be a daddy."

"What?" he whispered and took the test from me, staring down at it. "Fuck me."

I giggled. "Yeah, that's generally how it happens."

"Baby!" He pulled me into his arms and kissed me, his hand going to my neck as he laughed against my lips. "Holy shit, I'm gonna be a dad."

I grinned. "I know. It's so awesome."

Lifting me so I could wrap my legs around his waist, he carried me back into our bedroom. "I wondered why your tits were twice the size."

"They are not," I argued.

"You don't think?"

I glanced down at my chest. "No."

He dropped the stick on the floor (and me onto the bed) and tugged off my T-shirt. "I think I need to investigate closer."

"I haven't figured out dinner," I warned.

"I'm gonna eat you, baby, then we'll sort something else out."

I licked my lips as he ripped off his clothes and pulled me close. "I love you, baby."

"Love you too, honey."

My husband made love to me all night, our dinner of choice, pizza delivered within thirty minutes.

My world was complete and my life secure. Nothing could be better.

ABOUT PIPER

Piper Davenport writes from a place of passion and intrigue.

She currently resides in pseudonym-ia under the dutiful watch of the Writers Protection Agency, while living in Oregon with her husband.

Like Piper's FB page and get to know her!
(www.facebook.com/piperdavenport)

Made in the USA
Columbia, SC
17 January 2023